Carman

The Champion

Carman

The Champion

*The Story That Inspired
the Full–Length Motion Picture*

THOMAS NELSON PUBLISHERS®
Nashville

Published in Nashville, Tennessee, by Thomas Nelson, Inc.

Scripture quotations are from the KING JAMES VERSION.

ISBN 0-7852-6707-7

Printed in the United States of America.
1 2 3 4 5 6 QWD 05 04 03 02 01

I WANT TO DEDICATE THIS BOOK TO THE MEMORY OF MY brother Mario, who passed away May 2, 2000. You were always my hero, not because you were Chief of Police or because you won the medal of valor for extreme act of heroism or the combat cross, but because you taught me how to never be afraid of anything that was bigger than me and never be intimidated by a bully. When I see you again, I will bring another million souls with me. I will fight for them as you would have fought for me. You will never be forgotten.

Mario's little brother,
Carman

PROLOGUE

THE BLINDING LIGHTS OF TELEVISION CAMERAS AND exploding flashbulbs dazzled his eyes as, seemingly from a great distance, he heard the bell ring and began to move from his corner back into the ring. The crowd erupted into a sustained roar, and he had just enough time to wonder if this was how the gladiators of ancient Rome had felt on their way to certain death before his opponent was on top of him, punching tight and hard with the jabbing left hook that he'd been trying to avoid all night.

He bobbed out of the way, his ribs already aching from the pounding he'd been getting for eleven full rounds. He'd long ago given up the idea of a knockout, or even a TKO. What he wanted more than anything at this moment was to just last one more three-minute bout of brutality to reach the end of the fight. Let the judges sort it out from there. Then he would somehow find the strength to get back to the locker room where he could lie down, like a corpse on a slab, and let his pounding heart and pumping adrenaline slowly ease off. Then, maybe, he could get some sleep, even though he knew that when he woke again, the real pain would begin—every bruise and abrasion, every strained muscle and stretched ligament screaming out at the abuse it had been dealt.

Shaking the sweat out of his eyes, tinged red with the blood from the cut on his forehead that had almost stopped the fight, he blinked hard, trying to focus on the weaving figure in front of him. This guy was harder than he'd ever imagined; harder than his coach or his manager or any of the cigar-chomping handicappers who hung out down at the gym had ever given him credit for. No wonder he was the cruiserweight champion of the world. He was tough as a pit bull and could take as much punishment as he was dishing out.

But over the course of those eleven hard-hitting rounds, he had noticed something about his opponent: the slight but persistent tendency to leave himself open for a split second after he delivered the murderous left uppercut that had more than once left him dazed and disoriented. If he ever had a shot at taking this guy down, it would be at that precise moment, and the only way to make that happen was to leave himself open, one more time, for that vicious blow.

It was a plan that had all the simplicity and directness of desperation. He knew he'd held his own for the last thirty-plus minutes of fighting, but he wasn't sure it would be enough to give him the decision. In that moment, his thinking turned. He couldn't just endure the final round. He might never have such an opportunity again. He would try to end the fight. What he needed was to get close enough, fast enough, to lay in his own trademark roundhouse right. If the guy could survive that . . . well, then he deserved to keep his championship belt.

There was only one problem. He didn't know if he could hold up under another one of those uppercuts. His vision was already starting to blur, and he'd felt his knees buckle more than once after that nasty ninth round when he'd gotten the little impromptu surgery on his head and they'd called in the doctor.

Fortunately he had stopped the bleeding, but he knew that another hit anywhere near his head would open it up again, and if that happened, he could kiss the title good-bye.

His opponent made his move, a sudden flurry of abdominal punches that took the wind right out of him. The skirmish ended in a bear hug, and he hung on to the other fighter's sweating body for an extra moment as the referee tried to separate them, giving himself one more moment to prepare for what was coming.

Pulling apart, the two men stood facing each other, each on the ragged end of exhaustion, each pulling up his last shred of mental and physical stamina to keep standing beneath this relentless rain of blows. *It's now or never,* he told himself, and taking a deep breath, he moved in, deliberately dropping his shoulder to give the other boxer a clear shot at his jaw. He took the bait, and in the next second, as the uppercut landed hard and tight, he saw blackness begin to close in from all around. Reeling back, he fought the gravitational pull of the mat trying to drag him down, and with an intense surge of pure willpower, he pulled himself upright and blinked back the darkness. In the space between the ticking of the second hand in the arena, he saw, as clearly as if it were a photograph held up to his face, that he would have one, and only one, clear shot. Twisting his body at the hips to throw his full weight behind the punch, he let it go and, as if in slow motion, saw it connect, felt the heavy impact through the padding of his glove. Around him the roaring crowd seemed to suddenly go silent, and the man he had hit slid slowly down and out of his line of sight.

"One!" he heard the referee shout. "Two!" And the crowd's roar returned, louder than ever, ringing in his ears like the bells of a thousand cathedrals—all celebrating his victory. "Three! Four! Five!" From across the ring he could see his manager and his trainer jumping up and down, hugging themselves, and the exploding flashbulbs put black spots swimming before his eyes. "Six! Seven! Eight!" He couldn't feel his body, could hardly remember who he was or where he'd come from. All he knew for sure was that he was still standing and the other man was down and that was all that mattered. "Nine! Ten!" The crowd erupted into delirium, and he felt his arm being lifted high in the air as a disembodied voice came to him, announcing, "Ladies and gentlemen, the new cruiserweight champion of the world, Orlando Leone!"

He wished the referee would put his arm down. He wished the crowd would stop screaming. He wished he could go someplace that was quiet and dark and be by himself. But the chaos in the ring continued as fans and officials poured in through the ropes, all wanting to touch him, to be a part of the history he had just made. The roar that reached to the high ceiling of the arena grew louder and louder as hands from all sides grabbed at him and faces appeared suddenly before him, shouting and calling out his name. A robe was slipped over his shoulders, and he felt a strong grip on his shoulders helping to push him through the crowd.

At that moment his gaze fell for the first time on the prone body that still lay on the canvas. His opponent's face looked very pale, the blood that trickled from his mouth already beginning to coagulate in a puddle around his head. The doctor crouched nearby, his head laid on the unconscious man's chest.

"Is . . . he gonna be okay?" he managed to ask the doctor through his swollen lips.

The look the doctor gave him sent a cold chill up his spine. He watched numbly as the referee bent close and, a moment later, signaled frantically to officials on the sidelines. The last thing he saw, before being pushed out of the ring and up the steps toward the rear of the arena, was men in white coats rushing the other way, carrying a stretcher and an oxygen mask. It was an image that he believed would never be erased from his memory.

CHAPTER ONE

IT WAS A SOUND OF JOYFUL CELEBRATION, VOICES YOUNG and old, male and female, black, white, and in-between, lifted in harmony to celebrate and sanctify, a floor-shaking, window-rattling gospel choir letting loose at full throttle. "Our Father, who art in heaven," they sang as, behind them, a nine-piece combo picked up the rhythm and sent it soaring—bass, drums, guitar, keyboards, congas, and several rhythm instruments weaving in and out of the melody as they spurred the singers on to ecstatic new heights and the audience into a frenzy of exultant worship. "Hallowed be thy name. Thy kingdom come. Thy will be done." The spirit of the music echoed the conviction in the lives of all the people on the small stage of the urban youth center—lives salvaged and transformed and charged with victory and new purpose.

A large canvas hanging on the wall behind the choir was lit by a spotlight from the ceiling, and it rippled in the gentle night breeze that blew in from the wide-open windows. A hand stretched in agony was held to a piece of rough wood by a foot in a sandal. A heavy iron spike was poised above the hand with a hammer about to descend to drive it deep into the flesh. A single biblical quotation was spelled out beneath it—John 15:13—and for the uninitiated, the brutal depiction of crucifixion seemed jarringly out of place with the music that stirred souls and lifted spirits.

But for the young people gathered in the main hall of the youth center, there was no contradiction. Their faces, even now lifted up in the radiant light of pure devotion, bore the marks of life's harsh reality on the mean streets of the city. Here a teenage mother holding her infant; there a former gang member with a single tear tattooed in the corner of his eye; a Mohawked punk; a homeless denizen of the back alleys; an alienated kid from the suburbs—all of them understood that the price paid in the picture hanging above them was in real blood and actual human agony. There was nothing pretty about the death of the Man who hung on the cross, no pretending and no playacting. For everyone gathered there, nothing was more real than the One they called Jesus—His life, His death, His sacrifice, and His triumph.

As the music continued, reaching new crescendos at the end of each line in the Lord's Prayer, newcomers streamed into the hall, drawn like moths to the brilliant flame of new life. The crush of bodies, the throb of the music, the stomping feet and clapping hands, made the whole building shake on its foundations. A large, drafty sanctuary in the midst of the vast and faceless urban sprawl, the youth center seemed both timeworn and lovingly cared for. The furnishings from the 1970s, the flickering fluorescent lights, the threadbare carpet, and the creaking choir risers were old, but they were clean and everything was polished and scrubbed with pride and purpose. For many of the young people gathered there, the place was home . . . the closest they would ever come to feeling welcomed.

And because of that sense of familiarity and safety, the ones just now coming through the open double doors seemed to shed the wariness and weariness they carried with them through the streets to get there. Under the glare of the lights they seemed to suddenly become children again, acting their age, playfully shoving and scrapping with one another as a small and overworked cadre of volunteers tried their best to keep order. Through another doorway across the room, a noisy Ping-Pong match proceeded, while in the back of the hall, a team of young women served up punch and cookies to the senior citizens for whom the evening represented a rare night away from the dreariness of their cramped apartments and sad rest-home rooms. Toddlers set up a sympathetic wailing from the makeshift nursery, and children ran through the crowd, playing tag or simply letting off their excess of boundless energy.

Down a dimly lit hallway off the main entrance to the youth center was an oasis of quiet from the happy chaos and confusion of the evening service. The venetian blinds of the office windows let strips of faint light cross the crowded space with its clustered collection of mementos. It was a room that said a lot about the person who worked there. The bulletin board thick with messages and the piles of paper stacked in the "In" and "Out" boxes on the battered desk—all signified someone who knew how to work hard and didn't spare himself from the endless tasks that kept the youth center in operation.

But more than simply the office of a conscientious administrator, the room revealed a rich personal history, a time line that traced a career that seemed to reach to the very top of his calling. Faded photos of a fresh-faced young boy with dark curly hair standing in boxing trunks and gloves proudly holding up a Golden Gloves trophy; the same boy, now a young man, posing in nightclubs and the sparring rings of gyms with famous sports celebrities; a group shot of an American Olympic boxing team at an airport passenger lounge, the young athlete front and center and grinning ear to ear; the framed boxing fan magazine, with the young man, now fully grown, posed with a large shiny championship belt around his waist and a headline that read: "New Cruiserweight Champ."

As crowded as the wall was that tracked the rise of a true contender, the opposite wall was decorated in stark contrast with a single framed diploma. A certificate of ordination from a local Bible college, dated July 27, 1991, was made out in the name of *Orlando Leone*. It was a document set in a place of pride, the culmination of a long and often twisting road, the proof of a unique calling and destiny, and finally the answer to the question, What ever happened to that promising young boxer who once looked as if he might go all the way? The reality was, Orlando Leone had gone all the way . . . all the way to God.

Yet however far Orlando Leone might have traveled from the glory of the game, however much distance he might have put between himself and that twelve-round moment of truth played out in front of a roaring crowd screaming for blood, there was still some part of the man that could taste the thrill that came with victory and the bitter dregs that were the price of defeat. Orlando Leone was a boxer. It was in his blood, in the marrow of his bones.

That was why, as he walked down the hallway past his office, carrying a fresh tray of sandwiches for the snack table, he stopped suddenly, his ear attuned to a sound both far away and familiar—the roar of a crowd and the loud clang of the bell announcing the beginning of a new round. Orlando stood and listened for a moment, and anyone who walked by just then would have seen a man who might easily have climbed back into the ring—his body still toned and muscular, his eyes bright and alert, even his thick curly hair still full, with only the slightest flecks of gray at the temples. He moved with the natural grace of a boxer, shifting his weight effortlessly as if constantly sizing up an invisible opponent, looking for the opening, weighing his options.

But for all his catlike agility, there was nothing nervous or edgy in Orlando Leone's thirty-nine-year-old frame. Instead, his actions and movements seemed to originate from a calm center deep at his core, a place where he knew himself, his capabilities and skills, as much as he knew his weaknesses, the parts of his personality and character that needed the strength only a relationship with God could provide. In short, Orlando Leone was a man at peace with himself, his mission in life, and the higher purpose that guided each thought and every move.

After a moment, with the sound of the gospel celebration in the main hall still echoing down the corridor, Orlando set down the tray of sandwiches and followed the faint sounds of the boxing match down a short flight of stairs to the basement rec room of the youth center.

He pushed open the door onto a darkened space lit only by the ghostly glow of a television at which a dozen kids had gathered in rapt attention. On the screen was an image only too familiar to Orlando—brilliant lights illuminating a tiny square of rope and canvas on which two men moved toward each other, crouched low with the gloved fists protecting their faces. A quick flurry of punches sent up shouts and cheers from the crowd, the excited announcer gave a blow-by-blow account, and the kids gathered on the floor added their voices to the melee.

"Go for it! Go for it!"

"Man, Halbert is making hamburger of the champ!"

"One more right cross on Vasquez's glass jaw and it's all over!"

Orlando couldn't help smiling, a warm and genuine expression that seemed to light up his whole face. *Everyone's an expert,* he thought, and he moved into the room for a better look.

There was no question about it: a relentless fight to the finish was being played out before a worldwide audience for the heavyweight crown. And from what Orlando could see, after a quick perusal of the situation at the beginning of the eighth round, it looked odds on as if the champ was in no danger of losing his title. At two hundred and ten pounds of pure muscle, an obvious jump up from the days of one hundred ninety pounds, Orlando knew the game. He knew the tricks and he knew Vasquez. With speed and a light-footed dancing style that would have been remarkable for a man half his size, Antonio Vasquez was systematically chopping down Benji Halbert's tree, but only Orlando could see it. Backed up against the rope, crouched low and keeping his fists tight around his head, Halbert was defenseless against Vasquez's relentless punches to his torso. The blows came so fast, the champ's hands seemed to blur as he worked over every inch of his opponent's ribs and abdomen until the referee stepped in and pulled them apart.

The respite lasted only a moment before the punishment began again. If Orlando had to guess, he was sure they would have to call the fight by the end of the next round.

"That's his specialty," he said from his place in the shadows. Noticing his presence for the first time, the kids on the floor turned as one and stared at him, their eyes still bright from the glow of the television. "Body punching like that is Vasquez's specialty. He uses it to dismantle everybody he faces."

"You've seen the champ fight before?" one of the boys asked, his eyes as round as saucers.

"Seen him?" Orlando replied, keeping his chuckle to himself. "I used to spar with him, years ago, when he was first coming up. I showed him how to take apart a man's body, just like Marciano did. Then he started to use it against me when we were sparring. What a punk. I'll never forget how I used to feel after three rounds with him. Like someone had run over my chest with a truck."

The boys let out a collective gasp of awestruck wonder as the bell sounded and the round mercifully came to an end. At that moment Darla, a four-year-old girl with a tangle of curly hair and dark eyes, pushed open the door and announced solemnly, "Mr. Leone, your mama is looking for you. She says you should come right away."

Orlando smiled and held out his arms as the young messenger rushed toward him. Sweeping her up, he held her with gentleness that spoke of a whole other aspect to his character, worlds away from the boxing ring and its brutal test of human endurance. His love for this child, for all children, radiated from him like a halo and offered an irresistible attraction to any and all small people. They knew instinctively, sensing with the eyes of their hearts, that here, in a world of too many adults who wanted only to hurt them, was a grown-up they could trust.

"You go on back up there, sweetheart," he said to Darla, "and tell my mama I'll be there in just a minute."

"I don't know, Orlando," Darla replied, a look of serious doubt on her face. "She wanted to see you *now*."

"Just go tell her, then come right back," Orlando said, giving her a wink.

Orlando kissed the small voice of duty on the cheek and set her down, watching her scamper away as the bell sounded again and the boys turned their attention back to the fight. For the next several minutes they and Orlando traded opinions about the fight's progress, especially after the contender landed a series of well-placed shots to Vasquez's head.

"He's gonna lose it!" shouted one of the young voices from the floor. "He's throwing it all away."

"Not likely," replied Orlando, shaking his head. "He knows exactly what he's doing. He's just biding his time, setting himself up for the right opportunity. Trust me, he's figuring out Halbert's rhythm, working out the patterns of his hits. Vasquez will sneak right in between those elbows when he thinks he's covered up and lay him out. You watch."

As the drama of the fight continued to unfold, Darla scampered back up the stairs and ran down the corridor to the main hall where the gospel music had drawn to a close and the crowd stood in knots talking and sharing in the warm afterglow of the singing. She slowed down as she saw the formidable figure of Geneva Leone, Orlando's mother, a spry, feisty woman every bit as confident and assured as her son and with the added asset of the authority that comes with age. Wearing her curly white hair close cropped and dressed in a jogging suit and track shoes, Geneva looked as if she was ready for anything, and in her role as the youth center's chief enforcer and mother hen, she obviously took her duties very seriously. Breaking up a spontaneous game of jacks at the entrance to the hall, she simultaneously shut down a game of tag that was getting too rough, comforted a small boy who had skinned his knee, and gave a young mother with an infant the benefit of her child-rearing wisdom. Spotting the reluctant Darla across the room, she signaled her over.

"Did you find Mr. Leone, Darla?" she asked in an affectionate but no-nonsense tone of voice. "I need him up here right away."

Darla swallowed hard. "I told him, Miss Geneva," the child said with a quaver in her voice. "But he didn't come. He said he'd be here in a minute."

Geneva's severe look was directed over Darla's head to the

back of the hall, where a door led to the basement rec room. "Don't tell me," she muttered. "He's down there with those boys watching that fool boxing match."

Darla just stared back at her, her eyes two dark and secret pools. No matter what, she couldn't tell a tale on Orlando. Seeing the child's dilemma, the spry woman smiled and ran her long brown fingers through the little girl's thick hair. "You did good, honey," she said. "Now go on and play." She shot another look in the direction of the rec room door. "I'll take care of this myself." Instinctively, Darla ran back to where Orlando was.

As Geneva crossed the crowded hall, an older black man wearing a clerical collar set himself on a path to intercept her. "Geneva," he called when she was within hearing distance. "Geneva, hold up a minute." Geneva stopped, folding her hands across her chest as she waited for him to catch up with her.

"What is it, Simon?" she asked as he finally stood before her, slightly out of breath. "We've got the service starting soon, and I need to find my son. It ain't right to have a service without the founder of this joint. Mr. Leone should know that."

Simon smiled. "I'm looking for Orlando too," he said between gulps of air. "I need to ask him about the rummage sale we're supposed to be having next week." He chortled to himself. "But from the look on your face, I expect he'd be a lot happier to see me than he would be to see you."

"What's that supposed to mean?" snapped Geneva, and the man took a step backward, holding up his hands.

"Nothing," he insisted. "Nothing in the world, Mrs. Leone." He smiled, backing farther away. "If you find him, tell him I'm looking for him. That's all."

Geneva pushed forward, parting the crowd before her like an ocean liner in a crowded harbor. Opening the door that led to the basement stairwell, she heard the sounds of shouts and cheering coming from the darkness beyond. Sighing, she made her way down the steps and toward the flickering light of the television at the far end of the room.

Orlando and the boys watched as Vasquez unleashed a furious sequence of left and right hooks, moving relentlessly on his opponent like an avenging angel.

"Now, watch this, guys," Orlando was saying. "See how he's turning his feet in? That means he's getting ready to unload one of those monster roundhouse body shots. Here it comes!"

True to Orlando's prediction, Vasquez, his toes turned inward for added stability, delivered the inhuman blow. As an awestruck silence resounded through the arena, Halbert crumpled to his knees, then dropped, face first onto the floor. A split second later the rec room joined the faraway crowd in letting loose a tumultuous cheer.

"You called it!" shouted one of the boys. "It was like you were right there coaching him, Mr. Leone!"

"Oh, my son would have made a great coach," said Geneva dryly, and like guilty children caught in the act, they all turned to face her.

"Hi, Mom," Orlando said. "I was just . . ."

"He'd make almost as good a coach as he would a preacher. Which reminds me . . . ," Geneva continued, cutting off her son with a stern look. "You boys get yourselves upstairs. We've got a meeting starting"—she glanced at her watch—"in three minutes." She turned to Orlando. "And you, mister . . ."

"I'm on my way, coach" he answered, hurrying after the boys. "Hey, guys. Wait for me!"

As Orlando walked down the corridor toward the main hall, the raucous celebration that had launched the evening was quieting to a hushed expectation. The people had taken their places in long rows of folding chairs, talking in whispers as the overhead lights dimmed and the powerful pull of the music gave way to reverent anticipation—the main event was about to get under way.

Among the boys who now walked beside him like a squad of midget bodyguards, Orlando spotted a scrappy black kid in baggy pants and backward baseball cap. He was sparring with an invisible opponent and trying his best to emulate the stance and style of the champ he had just seen on television.

"Hey, Zack," Orlando said with a laugh as he placed a firm hand on the boy's head and directed him down the hall. "Let's save the title fight for another night. What do you say?"

Zack looked up sheepishly, then ran off to join his friends, just as Geneva caught up with her son, matching his long stride with her own. "I just don't know, Orlando," she said in a fretful tone of voice. "For a man who loves the Lord as much as you do, it seems to me you get just a little bit too much enjoyment out of watching two grown men beating up on each other." She shook her head. "Boxing is such a brutal sport. I can't help but wonder if it's healthy for the little ones to be watching."

Orlando reached over and put a comforting hand on his mother's shoulder. "Oh, come on, Mom," he replied. "Boxing's not nearly as rough as, say, football. It's just a sport like any other." He smiled. "Seems to me I can remember a time when you were right there in the stands, cheering me on."

Geneva wrinkled her nose at the distasteful memory. "I hated it then and I hate it now," she insisted. "Golf. Now that's a nice, safe way to let out your aggressions."

Orlando replied, "Mom, why does it always have to be about aggression? Do you have any aggression issues you want to share with your pastor?"

"Shut up, Orlando, or I'll give you a shot in the head," Geneva snapped back.

Orlando smiled as he said, "Oh, and you wonder where I get my aggression. What a mystery." But his face quickly darkened at the exchange as he struggled with his disturbing memories and the searing image of a man lying motionless and pale on a bloody canvas mat.

Noticing his sudden change of expression, Geneva spoke in a voice that had taken on a soft, compassionate tone. "Now you know that's not what I mean, Orlando," she said.

Hearing the concern behind her words, her son shook off the gloom that had come over him and, turning to his mother, gave her a loving smile. "That's okay, Mom," he said. "It's all behind me now." He looked up at the door to the main hall. In a moment they would walk through it and go down the aisle where hundreds of people had gathered to hear the words of life that their pastor would bring to them. "I've got other victories to win now," he added, and he gave her a squeeze around the shoulders. Together they emerged into the electric excitement of the crowded hall.

Encouraging cries of "Go for it, Pastor!" and "Preach it, brother!" greeted Orlando as he made his way toward the front of the room where a low stage was lit by a spotlight. Jumping onto it and stepping into the circle of white light, he grabbed the microphone that an assistant handed him and immediately turned his full attention, with an intense focus and complete concentration, on the crowd in front of him. It was time to do what he did best: pass along hope and faith and the confidence that came only from a personal relationship with a living Savior.

"You're looking good out there," he said as the crowd murmured happily. This was the moment they had waited all evening for. "Let me ask you a question," Orlando continued. "How many of you out there are ready to get your praise on?" A shout rose in response, and he put a hand to his ear. "What?" he said. "Maybe I'm going deaf in my old age, but I couldn't hear you. I said, how many of you are ready to get your praise on?" This time a roar went up, shaking the windows and echoing down the street into the cool city night.

"Well, then," Orlando shouted, "what are we waiting for?" At his signal, the band cranked it up behind him in the shadows and launched into a propulsive rendition of a gospel tune that was higher in velocity than the one they played before. Clapping his hands and singing along, Orlando felt a powerful presence begin to fill the room. *It never fails,* he thought. *You just have to ask, and He'll come.*

"Thank You, Jesus," he shouted and heard his words echoing in the voices of the hundreds gathered together, a single shout of glorious thanksgiving.

CHAPTER TWO

TWO HOURS LATER, THE LAST OF THE CONTENTED CROWD moved toward the exits, and a team of volunteers stacked the folding chairs and swept the floor clean. Orlando's clothes were still soaked from the sweat he had worked up by giving his all in the message for that evening. He sat on the edge of the stage, holding an earnest conversation with four-year-old Darla, who sat next to him, the curls of her dark hair catching the light from the overhead fixtures.

The affection that each felt for the other was obvious in the ease and confidence with which they spoke. Orlando knew well enough that his calling as the founder and chief shepherd of the youth center required him to show no favorites among the kids who looked to him for love and wisdom and protection. But he also knew that Orlando Leone was only human and that it would have taken someone with superhuman resolve to be able to resist Darla's large brown eyes, the special laugh she had when he said something funny, or the serious frown that came over her face when she was trying to understand something.

"So," Orlando was saying, "are you going to be ready to sing for us next week, Darla?"

The little girl nodded. "I've been practicing," she told him.

"Good for you," he replied. After a moment, he leaned over and said in a confidential tone, "You remember what I asked you about your mom, don't you?"

Darla's brow furrowed. "I . . . think so," she said hesitantly.

Orlando smiled. "I want you to tell her to come by and see me, Darla. So we can talk about that sculpture I want her to do. Can you remember that?"

Darla gave him a skeptical look. "Of course I can," she answered, then added proudly, "Mama says I'm very 'sponsible for my age."

Orlando hugged her. "I'm sure you are," he said, moving off the stage and helping her down. "Now you better get going. She's probably waiting for you right now."

"Okeydokey," chimed Darla, and Orlando watched fondly as she skipped away. When she was out of sight, he grabbed his jacket off the stage and turned to his mother, who was sitting in a folding chair nursing her evening cup of tea.

"Ready to go, Mom?" he asked.

"In a minute," she said, patting the chair next to her. "Come and sit with your old mother for a spell."

"Old?" Orlando laughed as he took the chair next to her. "I think you could give anyone in this place a run for his money, Mom."

"Maybe so," Geneva replied. "But right now what I'm more interested in is what you were talking to Darla about. Since when have you become an art collector?"

"Oh," said Orlando after a moment, "you mean the sculpture? I was going to tell you about that."

"How come I'm always the last to know what's going on around here anyway?" Geneva gently chided.

"There's really nothing to know, Mom," Orlando insisted. "I

was just thinking about how we might get investors interested, and I thought a good piece of sculpture, like a statue, might give them a point of identification."

"What kind of statue are you talking about?" his mother queried, clearly intrigued with the idea.

"Well," Orlando answered, "since it's going to be called the Orlando Leone Sr. Youth Center, I thought it would probably be best if it was a statue of Dad."

Geneva looked over at her son proudly. It was just like him to think of something like this, a way to bring honor to his father, to carry on the work that her husband had begun. "I think that's a wonderful idea, Orlando," she said.

"I hope so," he replied with a sigh. "I really need something to catch the attention of these moneymen. It's not easy trying to raise twenty million dollars."

"So . . . ," Geneva continued after a moment, and from the tone of her voice Orlando knew immediately she had something else on her mind, "you ever met this woman? How do you know she's a good enough artist?"

"I can't tell you that," her son answered. "But I do know she's a good mother. She's been dropping off Darla here on her way to work every day for the past eighteen months. And unless I miss my guess, I figure she's probably not getting rich carving statues. I figured she might be inclined to cut us a deal."

"That's my boy," said Geneva proudly. "Always thinking ahead." She punched him playfully on the shoulder. "Just don't get to thinking you're smarter than your mother. I've got a few years on you . . . and a lot more experience."

"Yes, ma'am," replied Orlando with a smile, then looked at his watch. "I'd sure like to get the benefit of that experience, but I'm going to be late for work as it is." Kissing Geneva on the cheek, he hurried to the exit door as she watched him go, her eyes alight with all the mixed emotions a mother feels for her child, from pride to protection to the unfailing maternal instinct that knows best for her baby, no matter how old he might be.

By the time Orlando stepped into the city night, standing on the steps of the youth center for a moment to take a deep breath of the cool air and scan the skyline of the city he called home, the street had nearly emptied of the crowd that had gathered earlier. It had been a long night, but it wasn't over yet and Orlando had to walk briskly to the corner and down the block to the bus stop in order not to miss his ride downtown. It was a routine he had been following for the better part of seven years, and tonight, as tired as he was, he wasn't about to neglect the important part of the routine.

"Lord," he prayed under his breath as he waited for the bus to arrive, "I thank You for the opportunity to serve You every day. And I thank You for the job You've given me to support myself." Orlando was more than a little familiar with the fact that even the apostle Paul had made tents to provide money so that he could feed and clothe himself during his years of ministry. If it was good enough for Paul, it was surely good enough for Orlando Leone.

After a few minutes the bus pulled to a stop, and the doors opened with a *hiss*. "Hey, Champ," said the driver with a smile as Orlando climbed aboard and his token clinked into the box by the steering wheel.

"Hey, Wayne," Orlando replied. "Almost right on time, as usual."

"We do our best, Orlando," the driver answered even as he steered the bus back into traffic and pointed it toward the bright lights of the skyscrapers in the distance. Orlando took his usual seat halfway back on the nearly deserted bus and settled down with a deep sigh. It was the first time he'd had a chance to relax all day, but even now, tired as he was, he couldn't shut his mind off. It seemed that every thought carried a twenty-million-dollar price tag, and he once again turned over all the options and opportunities that had presented themselves, trying to find the right combination to make his dream come true.

But behind all the calculations, something troubled Orlando, and it wasn't until the bus pulled up at his stop outside a luxurious downtown hotel that he was finally able to put his finger on it. His mother's comment, about the only sport worth playing being the one where someone got hurt, had been playing over and over in the back of his mind during the whole ride across the city. He knew she meant no harm, even though her words had cut deeply. *Oh, well,* he thought, *if she hadn't brought it up, something else would have reminded me of that fateful night and the fearful consequences that followed.* Something always did. It was a burden he carried with him everywhere, and as he waved good-bye to the bus driver, he threw up another silent prayer for the man he had almost killed with his fists.

The automatic door slid open as he approached, and he entered the opulent lobby of the hotel. Piano music tinkled from the bar, and everywhere well-dressed people drinking expensive cocktails sat in overstuffed chairs. At the far end of the atrium, a wedding party had gathered. At the other end, doctors from a conference in the grand ballroom were talking shop. A lavish sweet-sixteen birthday party was breaking up, and he could see several young people emerging from the ballroom where a youth convention had just let out for the evening. It was another five-star night in the city's most prestigious hotel.

Waving to the receptionists behind the counter, Orlando entered a door marked EMPLOYEES ONLY and made his way down a long hall to a small room crowded with surveillance monitors showing various views of hallways, rooftops, and basement rooms—the nerve center of the hotel's security operation.

Sitting at the console that controlled the screens was a pudgy black man in a tight-fitting uniform, his feet resting on the rim of the board and a bowl of cereal resting on his ample stomach. As Orlando slipped on a tie and a blue blazer with the hotel's emblem on the pocket, he noticed that the guard occasionally glanced up at the screens, but seemed more intent on scooping up the last few bits floating in the milk at the bottom of his bowl.

"Well, Dexter," said Orlando. "Looks like it's just you and me on the late shift tonight." He smiled. "But maybe I got that wrong. Looks like you brought your best friends with you."

Dexter looked up with a guilty grin. "Fruit Loops," he said sheepishly. "My favorite."

"Let me ask you something, Dex," Orlando continued, sitting down in another chair near the console and, punching a series of buttons, giving the hotel a quick scan through its security cameras. "Is there anything that you put in your mouth that's not your favorite?"

The guard seemed to be giving the question serious consideration when Orlando reached over and pushed his feet off the console.

"Hey," protested Dexter. "What did you do that for?"

"Because I've got to work here, Dexter," Orlando replied. "And your feet aren't exactly a vase of roses."

"I changed my socks last week, boss," the guard insisted.

"That's good, Dex, but maybe next week you'll change into a clean pair," Orlando said and nodded. "Now if you can just get it through your head that I didn't hire you to be a taster for a cereal company, we'll be getting somewhere." He pointed at the screen. "See," he continued, "you're supposed to be watching up here, making sure nobody steals a couch or falls out a window. Then if you do a good job, you get yourself a break. You can go to the employees' lounge and eat all the cereal you want." He slapped Dexter on the back. "That's the rules, buddy. And around here, we live by the rules."

Dexter nodded and set his bowl on the floor beside his chair. He looked dutifully up at the screen while Orlando made an entry in the evening log, interrupted after a moment by Dexter's excited voice.

"Boss," he said, "I think we got us a situation up at the reception desk."

Orlando quickly fixed on a screen showing an agitated man berating a cashier, waving his hands, and wagging his finger. "Be right back," Orlando said and dashed out of the room.

Five minutes later he found himself arbitrating a billing discrepancy with a guest whose English was none too intelligible. "Italiano?" Orlando asked after a moment, and when the man nodded eagerly, Orlando spoke to him in perfectly inflected Italian, resolving the problem and even receiving an invitation to visit Naples on his next trip to the mother country. Even though the Leones were from Sicily, he graciously accepted.

It was all in a night's work for Chief Security Officer Orlando Leone, but the night had only just begun. Walking back toward the surveillance center, he glanced out the front entrance in time to see the familiar face of a neighborhood homeless man loitering under the awning of the sweeping circular driveway. As Orlando crossed to the doors, a group of teenagers exited the hotel directly in front of the homeless man.

"Got some change?" the indigent asked, holding out his hand to the kids as Orlando stepped outside.

The embarrassed teens made a wide berth around the beggar,

and Orlando moved in, putting himself between the homeless man and the hotel guests. "How are you doing, Sigmund?" he said, putting his arm around the dusty and threadbare jacket on the man's shoulders.

"Oh, I guess I'll survive, Champ," the homeless man answered. "Sure am hungry, though."

As if on cue, Dexter suddenly appeared from the valet parking booth, carrying a large sandwich in both hands. "Everything okay here, Orlando?" he asked in his most official voice. "Need any help?"

"As a matter of fact," Orlando answered, "I do." He held out his hand. "Let me see that sandwich, Dex."

"This sandwich?" asked the mystified guard as he looked down at it. "Well, I guess I can spare you a bite," Dexter grumbled while he grudgingly passed over the hulking sandwich. "But that's my predinner snack and I—hey!" The guard watched in dismay as Orlando passed the food to the homeless man.

"That should do you for the night, Siggy," he said.

"Thanks," Sigmund replied gratefully, taking a large mouthful of meat, cheese, and bread.

"Bu . . . but . . . that . . . ," Dexter stammered.

"You ain't got no viruses or anything, do you, Dex?" asked Orlando with a wink toward the homeless man.

"What are you talking about, man?" sputtered the outraged guard as Orlando clapped the shabby man beside him on the back.

"Don't worry," Orlando said, trying hard not to laugh. "My friend here assures me you won't catch any diseases from eating his predinner snack. At least no fatal one, that is."

"Real funny, Orlando," muttered Dexter. "I'm dying of laughter."

"That's better than dying of exploding," Orlando quipped before turning back to the homeless man. "Now listen, Sig," he said kindly. "I don't want you out here bothering these nice boys and girls anymore. When you start messing with them, they get scared. Understand?"

"They're scared of me, Champ?" asked this denizen of the streets in disbelief.

"Nothing personal," Orlando assured him. "It's just that . . . well, they've never been up close and personal with someone of your wide experience and understanding of the streets before."

Sigmund nodded sagely. "Sure," he said. "I can understand how that might give them pause."

"You have a nice night," Orlando told him. Leaning in close, he added in a confidential tone, "You come around the kitchen entrance tomorrow morning, and I'll make sure the chef cooks you up a nice breakfast."

"Sure thing, Champ," said the man around a mouthful of sandwich as he moved down the driveway and into the night. "Many thanks, and the Lord bless you."

Orlando watched him go as, behind him, he could hear Dexter muttering under his breath. "Is there a problem, Dex?" he asked, turning around at last to face him.

"I made that sandwich special," protested Dexter, pointing at the retreating figure of the homeless man. "It had provolone, and you know how much I like provolone, Orlando."

"Dexter, old buddy," said Orlando as the two of them walked back into the lobby, "I've got two words for you."

"And what might they be?" Dexter asked cautiously.

"*Slim Fast,*" Orlando answered.

"You wasted your talents on boxing," Dexter moaned as they headed back to the security office. "You're a born comedian."

Eight hours later, Orlando found himself sitting on his usual red vinyl stool at the counter of the all-night diner where he stopped for a cup of coffee and a bran muffin on his way home. His head drooping and his eyes red-rimmed, Orlando chased the same thought around in his exhausted brain that always came to him at this hour of his endless day. *How much longer can I keep this up?* he asked himself, the image of a candle lit at both ends swimming up in his fatigued imagination.

Boyd, the burly counterman, had seen his customer like this before—nearly every morning, in fact, since Orlando had taken the security job at the hotel up the street several years ago. Knowing better than to start a conversation until Orlando had had at least two cups of java, Boyd silently poured a second serving of the thick black liquid and, following another well-established routine, carefully laid out a copy of the sports section from the early edition of the city's daily newspaper.

Orlando's tired eyes fell on the banner headline sprawled across the top of the page: "Vasquez Holds On to the Heavyweight Crown: News Conference Set to Name Next Contender."

"I guess this means we'll be having to put up with his mouth for quite a while," observed Orlando with a sigh.

"What do you mean, Mr. Leone?" asked Boyd, topping off the coffee.

Orlando looked up and smiled weakly. "Oh, nothing, Boyd," he replied. "Just a sick thought I had. I'm praying it off me."

"I hear you." Boyd nodded. "I guess the champ grew himself a big head along with those big muscles." He leaned forward, his elbows on the table. "Tell me something, Mr. Leone," he asked. "When you were in the game, you ever run into Antonio Vasquez?"

Orlando nodded. "Lots of times," he admitted. "My last year, I was training to make the move from cruiserweight to heavyweight. His trainer used to bring Vasquez down from Minneapolis pretty regularly to spar with me. Back then he had a reputation as a real pile driver, knocking out everyone in the amateurs, one after the other, just like Tyson used to do." He smiled at the recollection. "I smacked him around pretty good, though. Taught him a little respect if you know what I mean." He shook his head, dispelling the memories of past glories. "But, hey, that was more than ten years ago, a lifetime in that game."

"So I guess you could probably predict all his moves," said Boyd with admiration in his voice.

"Oh, yeah. I taught him a few of them myself. Wish I hadn't now."

"Do you think anyone can beat him?" Boyd asked.

"Truthfully, no," replied Orlando.

"But he's so predictable," countered Boyd. "He comes straight at you."

Orlando smiled and said, "Just like a tornado ripping through a trailer park. He's a real force of nature. The question is not, Is he predictable? The question is, What are you gonna do about it? The answer is, Nothing. Nothing but get tore up from the floor up." Taking a final gulp of coffee, Orlando pulled out a few bills and slapped them on the counter. "You have a good day now, Boyd," he said. "The Lord bless you."

The sun was well up over the concrete canyons of the city as Orlando made his way to the bus stop, hardly noticing the roar of traffic on the elevated roadway he passed under on his way home. There, in the early morning snarl of honking horns and squealing brakes, Alicia Corbin maneuvered across lanes and around stalled cars with all the skill and ability of a boxer in the ring. A mass of dark curls framed the olive-skinned oval of her face, with its high intelligent forehead and clear brown eyes that sparkled with lively energy and just a hint of mischief. Alicia

Corbin was a woman determined to get the most out of every moment of her life, no matter what came her way. For her, every challenge was an opportunity in disguise, up to and including being a single mother. She threw a quick glance into the backseat where her daughter, Darla, sat watching the scenery slip past, the sun glinting off the towering skyscrapers and the high clouds making fanciful shapes as they drifted by. Under her breath, Alicia once more thanked God—if there even was such a thing—for bringing Darla into her life. She might not have been sure about much, but she knew one thing from the very depth of her soul. Her little girl was a blessing from heaven, an angel sent to bring light and laughter into her life.

Sitting beside Alicia in the aging but well-tended car was a brash black woman talking too loudly into a cell phone. "Well, did he hit you, or didn't he?" she demanded to know while at the same time drumming her polished fingernails impatiently on the dashboard. She listened for a moment longer, then in a sudden rush of words shouted into the phone, "Girl, you've got to get your act together! Why in the world would you want to move in with some guy who's hitting you upside the head one day and telling you he's in love with you the next?"

She cupped her hand over the phone. "Sorry, sweetie," she said to Alicia. "This girl ain't got the sense of a doorknob."

Alicia smiled. "Don't worry, Kathleen," Alicia replied. "I'm sure she's counting her lucky stars she's got a social worker who's as kind and compassionate as you are."

Kathleen shot her a sideways look, unsure whether her best friend was teasing or not, then, hearing something on the other end of the line, returned to berating her hapless client. "Now you listen to me," she said. "You move in with the no-good scrub, and you're asking for more of exactly what you've been getting."

Alicia shook her head in mock exasperation and, looking again in the rearview mirror at her four-year-old daughter, asked, "So . . . did he say anything else to you, sweetheart?"

Darla fixed her gaze on her mother's eyes in the mirror. "He said to be sure to tell you that he wanted to talk to you, Mama," she said in a high, chiming voice.

"I know, Darla," Alicia replied. "You already told me that . . . three times. But was there anything else? Like how much he had to spend or anything like that?"

Darla's brow knitted as she thought for a long, hard moment. "He was real nice!" she said suddenly, her face brightening.

"Honey," Kathleen was saying sternly into the phone, "you listen to Kathleen. No one's got your interests at heart like I do and you know that. I'm going to come down there this afternoon and have a talk with this Leone character myself." She listened for a moment before interrupting. "No," she said, "don't try to talk me out of it. I'll see you later. I've got to make another call." Cutting the connection, she heaved a dramatic sigh. "These teenage mothers," she complained, rolling her eyes. "Sometimes they ain't got the sense of a flea."

Alicia gave her a sidelong look. "I thought you had to make another call," she said.

"I lied," Kathleen replied, then turned quickly to Darla in the backseat. "Sometimes Aunt Kathleen has to tell her clients things that aren't exactly true, sweetie," she told the child. "But that doesn't mean you should lie. You know what the tenth commandant says: 'Thou shalt not lie.'"

Alicia suppressed a laugh. "Oh," she said, "and since when is Aunt Kathleen so spiritual?"

Kathleen reached into her purse and, pulling out a tube of lipstick, started applying it while looking in the visor mirror. "Never you mind," she replied haughtily. "I know what's good for that little girl." She turned to face her friend. "Besides, I've got to get lots of practice for when I meet up with this pastor disaster you're talking about. He's probably one of those real phony Holy Rollers, I'll bet."

"Oh," replied Alicia, "I'm sure he's not all that bad."

"And what makes you so sure?" countered Kathleen. "You have never met him, have you?"

"Well, no," Alicia answered uncertainly. "But—"

"Let me tell you, honey," Kathleen interrupted, twisting her lipstick closed and putting it back in her bag. "The so-called men of God are all the same. A bunch of hypocrites, always peddling their pie in the sky and catchin' money on the fly. If all the answers to life were so easy, all I'd ever have to do is tell all those preteen mothers who come into my office every day that Jesus loves them and that would make them right as rain."

"'Jesus Loves Me!'" Darla piped in from the backseat. "We sing that song every day!"

"That's nice, Darla," said her mother before turning her attention back to Kathleen. "I'm not saying Jesus is the answer or anything," she continued. "I'm just saying . . . well, it would be nice to have something spiritual in our lives. I'll bet even your clients might agree with that."

"You just watch yourself," Kathleen warned. "And you watch your little girl too." She sniffed. "You ask me, you're making a big mistake letting Darla get involved in any kind of church group, no matter how much they say they're just trying to help you out. They've got weird ideas, Alicia. You listen to me. They're all freaks."

"Oh, please," Alicia replied, rolling her eyes. "As far as I can tell, they haven't scheduled any alien abductions between the

Ping-Pong and sing-alongs this week. But I'll be sure to let you know if they do."

"You can make fun all you want," Kathleen said. "We'll just see who gets the last laugh."

"I like to laugh!" Darla interjected from the back, and for a moment, their disagreements forgotten, all three started to giggle.

CHAPTER THREE

ALICIA'S CAR PULLED UP TO THE FRONT OF THE YOUTH center, which even at the early morning hour was already a hub of activity. Other parents were dropping off their children for the day care program, while street kids played an impromptu game of hoops on a makeshift court at the side of the old building. The sun had burned away the evening mists, and the whole scene was cast in a warm and glowing light. Here was a place where people could come to feel safe from the mean streets all around them; a temporary haven for those who had never known the comfort of a caring home; a small slice of sanity in a cold and uncaring world.

To make the confusion outside the center even worse, a huge garbage truck was making its rounds down the street and, with its back-up lights blinking, started moving in reverse straight toward Alicia's car.

"Oh, great," she said in frustration. She hit the gearshift and, turning around, steered the car out of the way. "I'm already late for work and this guy's about to run me over."

"Look," said Kathleen, glancing around dubiously at the passing kids on the street, some of them arrayed in gang colors. "You stay here. Make sure nobody tries to steal your car." She grabbed a packet of papers off the front seat. "I'll run your brochure in to

Mr. High and Mighty. If he can afford to hire you, then he can give you a call, just like any other customer would."

Alicia looked over to her friend doubtfully. "Well," she said after a moment, "all right." She put her hand over Kathleen's. "Just try for once to be nice, okay? I really could use the work."

"You know me," said Kathleen with an angelic smile.

"Yeah," answered Alicia with a smile. "I know you a little too well." She turned in her seat and gestured for her daughter to come up and give her a kiss.

"Bye, honey," she said as she felt the child's small arms around her neck. "You have a wonderful day. Mommy will be back this afternoon."

"I love you, Mommy," said Darla. "And don't worry. I'll make sure Orlando says a special prayer for you."

"See what I'm talking about?" demanded Kathleen as she opened the door and stepped into the warm sunshine. "Once they start praying with these kids, it's all over."

Alicia watched as her friend took Darla by the hand and hurried across the street. *Maybe Kathleen is right,* she thought. *Maybe all this God stuff is putting dreams and fantasies into my daughter's head.* But she couldn't remember when her child had seemed happier and more content. Somebody must be doing something right, she had to admit. She could only hope that, whoever it was, he'd keep it up. For Darla's sake and for hers.

Inside the center, the happy confusion and bustling activity were even more intense than on the street outside, and the echoing sounds of playing children bounced off the walls and added to the general sense of barely controlled pandemonium. With Darla as her guide, Kathleen let herself be led across the main hall to the corridor where Orlando's office door stood half open. Knocking to announce her presence, she heard a sleepy stirring on the other side and, pushing her way in, saw a figure rising from the sofa. Running his fingers quickly through his hair, he opened the blinds to lighten the room.

"Hello," Orlando said, his voice still a little thick with sleep. "Hey, sweetheart," he added as he saw Darla running to hug him. "And you must be . . ." He stopped, confused by the obvious discrepancy between the little girl and the woman who held her hand. "Darla's mother?" he finished as his words trailed off.

"Do I look like this little girl's mother?" Kathleen snapped back, one hand on her hip.

"Well, no," confessed an embarrassed Orlando. "It's just . . . I was expecting—"

"Never mind what you were expecting," Kathleen interjected. "I am Alicia's best friend, and I never did a sculpture in my life." She lifted her chin proudly. "I am a social worker. I sculpt with my words!"

"This I can see," Orlando replied. He yawned and started to rub the sleep from his eyes.

"I'm sorry," continued Kathleen with a contemptuous look. "I hope I didn't interrupt your nappy time."

"No, no," replied Orlando, raising his hands. "I just got off work a few hours ago and thought I might . . . well, that's not important." He looked past Kathleen to the open door. "So, will Alicia be coming by . . . ," he began swallowing hard, "anytime soon?"

"I should say not!" countered Kathleen. "My friend is a very busy lady. In fact, I'm not at all sure she'll even have time to consult with you, much less actually take on your little project here." She reached in her purse and pulled out the brochure she had taken off the front seat of the car, then added, "But she did want me to drop this by. Just in case."

The phone rang, and with an apologetic look Orlando crossed

to the desk to answer it. He couldn't tell why, but he was pretty sure this formidable woman had taken a dislike to him. It was something he was going to have to get to the bottom of, as soon as he took care of whoever was on the other end of the line.

"Leone here," he said into the receiver.

"Hey, buddy," replied the voice at the other end, and Orlando knew immediately that the call was from his lawyer and long-time friend from the old neighborhood, one of the few people in Orlando's life who had stuck with him through thick and thin and all the changes that had come over the past few years.

"Hey, Pete," he said, eyeing Kathleen across the room. "Can I call you back? I'm kind of in the middle—"

"Pop quiz, hot shot," Pete interrupted as if he hadn't heard a word. "When were you and I supposed to meet with McCracken and Sons, Contractors?"

"I've got it down for . . . wait a minute," he said, resting the receiver on his shoulder and rifling through the papers on his cluttered desk.

While the phone conversation unfolded, Kathleen had a chance to take a quick look around the office. Her eyes passed over the children's drawings taped up everywhere and lingered on the mementos of Orlando's boxing days, the gloves and trophies. Although the framed clippings on the walls looked intriguing, she wasn't able to study them before she heard a deep groan coming from across the room.

"Oh, brother," said a chagrined Orlando. "It was supposed to be today, wasn't it?"

"'Supposed to be' is the key phrase, my friend," said Pete over the line. "If I were you, I'd try a little harder to keep important appointments like these, Leone."

"I know, I know," Orlando answered. "It's just that these night shifts are really taking it out of me." He signaled across the room to Kathleen: he'd be with her in just a minute.

At that moment, Kathleen noticed a photograph of Orlando with his arm around Sugar Ray Leonard. More to herself than to Orlando, she said, "Ooh. Now that's one fine man. If he ran this center, I might join myself."

But Pete, calling from his downtown office, didn't seem in any hurry to end his conversation with Orlando. "I'm sure McCracken and Sons would be very sympathetic to your situation," he continued. "That is, if they were the sympathetic types. Come on," he cajoled his friend, "get serious. You need these guys. I've already told you, they're the only contractors I could find who would even agree to look at your proposal. Nobody in his right mind would think twice about remodeling a broken-down old hospital to the tune of twenty million dollars. Especially since you don't exactly have that kind of cash sitting in your savings account. That is, unless you won the lottery and haven't told your old friend."

"Get another meeting," Orlando pleaded. "Tell them anything you want, just get them back into your office. I'll be there. I promise."

He hung up the phone just in time to see Kathleen take one of the pamphlets he had prepared about the youth center and its services off his desk and slip it into her purse. *Strange,* he thought quickly, *if she wanted it, I would have been happy to give her one.* But as a pastor, Orlando had learned a long time ago that, when it came to religion, people were easily spooked. Which was why, as much as he could manage, he avoided all the rules and regulations that went along with faith in God. Those would come later. What mattered first was that people met Jesus, face-to-face and heart-to-heart.

He looked at his watch realizing, as usual, that it was later than he thought. "You'll have to excuse me," he muttered as he moved toward the door and out into the hallway. Looking over his shoulder, he saw that Kathleen was following close behind, still holding on to Darla's hand. "So," he said, trying to make conversation, "you're a social worker?"

"That's right," answered Kathleen, looking around the busy center as they walked. "And I take it you run this little operation around here?"

"Well, I try." Orlando sighed. "Most times, though, it ends up running me."

"Can I play now?" asked a plaintive Darla, tugging at Kathleen's hand.

"Of course you can," replied Kathleen, letting the child go and watching her skip off to join a group of friends.

Orlando had reached out and stopped another little girl who was happily playing tag in the hallway. "Have you seen my mom, Rachel?" he asked.

"She's in the rec room," the girl responded, pointing the way before running off to her game.

"Do you mind if I ask you a question?" Kathleen inquired.

"Would it matter if I did?" he quipped.

She smiled in spite of herself. "What do the parents of these kids think about what you're doing here?" she asked.

Orlando looked at her with a curious expression. "What do you mean?" he wondered.

"Well," Kathleen answered, folding her arms confrontationally, "you seem real good at enforcing all this religious stuff with these young people, telling them what to think and how to act. Isn't that a little bit out of line?"

I knew it, Orlando thought. *This one's got a problem with author-*

ity figures—especially God. He'd spotted it a mile away. "Let me try and explain," he said, even though he was pretty sure he wasn't going to make much headway with her. "First of all, I don't think teaching kids the difference between right and wrong is going to inflict any permanent harm on them. In fact, this is probably one of the only places in this city where they might get a chance to even know that there is a difference." He stopped and turned to face Kathleen directly. "But more important than that, what I teach them is not 'religious stuff.' Christianity is not a religion. Not in the way you mean it. Christianity is a relationship. Between you and your Creator. Besides," he added with a smile, "everybody believes in something. I bet you believe that when you get up in the morning, the floor is still going to be under your feet and the roof is going to be over your head. Same thing with me. I believe God is there for me and for everyone who takes Him at His word. It's something I've come to depend on."

Kathleen opened her mouth to respond, but at that moment a whirlwind of angry words and flying fists erupted down the hall. Crossing quickly, Orlando got between two teenage boys throwing wild punches and shouting slurs against each other's mother. Holding them apart at arm's length, he gave the clear, crisp order: "Cool it!"

"Get your hand off me, old man," said the taller boy, whose baseball cap had been knocked askew on his head during the tussle. Backing away, he raised his fists again. "You want a piece of this, dude? Huh? Do you?"

Throwing a fast jab at Orlando, he was surprised to find his blow effortlessly blocked. Coming at him with another, Orlando ducked, and the kid was suddenly surprised to find his opponent nowhere in sight. It was then that he felt a steel-strong pair of arms come up around his chest, holding him tightly in a bear hug.

"Maybe you didn't hear me the first time," Orlando repeated evenly. "I said to cool it."

"Yeah," the helpless teen whined, "but he started it. You should have heard what he said about my mother."

Orlando turned to the other youth. "Did you dis his mother?" he asked severely.

"Yeah," protested the second teen. "But he was saying the same thing about mine."

"That's enough, both of you," Orlando said, letting his captive go. "I thought I told you both that a real man never talks down about a woman . . . especially someone's mother." He looked around him where a small crowd of wide-eyed children had gathered to watch the fracas. "You want these kids growing up to talk trash like you two?" he asked, putting on his most solemn face. "This is God's house. We treat everyone with respect here. And don't you forget it. Now," he said, turning to the tall teen, "I want you to apologize to your homeboy here."

When the kid muttered something under his breath, Orlando stepped up until they were nearly nose to nose. "I can't hear you," he loudly remarked.

"I'm sorry," said the teen.

At Orlando's command, when the second boy echoed the apology, he had the boys shake hands and sent them off. As they left, he added, "Go shoot some hoops and not each other!" For Orlando Leone, it was all in a day's work, but he couldn't help noticing, with just a hint of satisfaction, the impressed look on Kathleen's face.

From across the room, he spotted Geneva and, smiling at his guest, said, "I need to talk to my mother for a moment. Would you excuse me?"

"Take your time," she replied airily. When he was halfway

across the room, she whipped out her cell phone and punched a rapid succession of numbers.

"Hello?" Alicia answered after one ring.

"It's me," said Kathleen.

Alicia sighed into the phone. "If I'd known it was going to take this long—" she began.

"Sorry, honey," Kathleen interrupted. "They've been having one crisis after another around here. From the sound of it, I'd have to guess he was talking to his lawyer on the phone. He had that taking-care-of-business tone of voice. And there were some kids having it out in the hall. I'm telling you, these religious people are a few tacos shy of a combination plate if you know what I mean."

"Never mind that," Alicia insisted, still sitting in the stalled traffic. "Did you give him the brochure? Is he interested in hiring me?"

"I really couldn't say," Kathleen admitted. "I can't seem to get a word in edgewise."

"You can't?" Alicia said, and Kathleen could hear the wry tone in her voice. "That's quite a dilemma, coming from you."

"Yeah, very funny," she snapped. "Listen, I'm telling you, there's something off about this guy. He started preaching at me right out of the blue for no reason. And besides, what kind of a job is running a youth center for a grown man anyway?"

"I don't care what kind of man he is," Alicia warned her friend. "You just make sure he knows I'm available to work."

"Oh, sure," Kathleen retorted sarcastically. "Like he's got a dozen other sculptors lined up who are just dying to do his funky little job for him." She snorted. "Guy's probably paying peanuts on top of everything else. I'm telling you. You really want this job, you got it." She saw Orlando returning and spoke hurriedly into the phone. "Got to go. He's coming back." She smiled sweetly as Orlando approached. "Disaster averted?" she asked.

"Oh," replied Orlando, returning her smile. "I wouldn't say averted exactly. More like postponed."

"Are you always functioning in crisis mode around here?" Kathleen asked.

Orlando shrugged. There was no point in hiding the obvious. "We kind of fly by the seat of our pants," he admitted. "Money and resources are very tight." He sighed. "There are so many needs and so few people who are willing to help."

"Oh, I doubt that," Kathleen responded sharply. "You religious types are always good at talking people into handing over their precious time and hard-earned money."

Orlando looked at her through narrowed eyes. "Let me ask you something," he said. "Are you always this charming, or are you just trying to impress me?"

Kathleen started to open her mouth in reply before she realized, to her surprise, that she had no snappy comeback to deliver.

"Come on," Orlando said with a smile as he noticed her tongue-tied situation. "I'll walk you to the front door."

Still sitting in her car, Alicia saw Kathleen emerge onto the front stoop of the youth center, deep in conversation with Orlando. Alicia watched intently as the two continued their talk, noting with satisfaction that he was holding her brochure in his hand. *At least Kathleen got that part right,* she thought.

"You know, Kathleen," Orlando said, unaware of the eyes that watched him from across the busy avenue, "most of the parents who bring their kids here to us are thrilled just to see that there's someplace they can come that keeps them off the street. Maybe they're not all as brainwashed by religion as you might think."

"Maybe, maybe not," was Kathleen's cynical reply. "Maybe they just don't have any other alternatives. Did you ever think of that?"

The two paused a moment as three teens in full gang regalia sauntered down the street while pedestrians parted fearfully. "Oh, there are alternatives, Kathleen," Orlando countered. "They're just not as healthy . . . or as holy."

"Whatever you say, Pastor," she replied tersely. She looked across the street and saw Alicia staring at them. "I guess I better get going. You've probably got a bunch of souls to save or something." She stuck out her hand. "It's been a real pressure meeting you," she quipped.

"Likewise," Orlando shot back. "Please drop by again . . . when you can't stay as long."

Kathleen's parting glance summed up all her doubt and hostility toward this man and his mission. As she hurried across the street, she remembered the pamphlet she had taken off his desk. She pulled it out of her purse as soon as she was in the car and stuffed it into Alicia's. "Read it later and gag," she said as Alicia pulled into the stream of traffic. "You should be listening to me, girlfriend. First of all, he's one of those religious nuts, just like I told you. And second, I don't think he's got two dimes to rub together, much less pay your fee for putting together a sculpture."

Alicia listened silently. Orlando Leone seemed engrossed in the brochure that Kathleen had given him, illustrated with Alicia's artistry—artistry she hoped might make a connection.

CHAPTER FOUR

THE VIEW FROM THE PENTHOUSE SUITE WAS SPECTACULAR. The city nightscape spread out like a picture postcard, and in the distance, the lights of huge cargo ships in the harbor seemed to move like elephants in a circus, waiting for their turn to dock.

Inside the suite, a complimentary basket of fruit had been set on the coffee table, and next to the remains of an elaborate room service dinner, a bottle of pricey French champagne was cooling in a silver bucket. Fresh flowers adorned every room. No detail in any of the rooms had been left to chance. This was high living at its best.

But the man huddled on the overstuffed sofa didn't seem to be enjoying his plush surroundings. In fact, he hardly seemed to notice them at all. A fine sheen of sweat glistened on his forehead, and each random sound from the hallway outside caused him to start with fear, his eyes bulging in their sockets and his hands trembling as he tried to light a cigarette.

Without warning, the door to the suite burst open with a savage kick from an oversized thug in a shiny sharkskin suit. A huge diamond ring on his little finger reflected the morning light. Standing next to him was another specimen of gangland muscle. The man on the sofa jumped to his feet, looking desperately for a way out, but the enforcers entered the suite and, after a quick check, parted to let their boss come through the doorway.

Immaculately dressed in a custom-tailored suit, the man strode in as if he had long been accustomed to all the trappings of absolute power and fear that he inspired. His eyes were as cold as those of a reptile, and his thin lips were curled into a perpetual sneer. The look on his face sent a single, terrifying message: here was a man who was capable of doing anything and everything to another human being, and he would take real pleasure in the process.

The man in the room whimpered softly as the other man approached him, stopping only to pick up the champagne bottle and admire its vintage. Handing it to one of his strong-arms, he gestured for the big guy to open it and then, with a flourish, sat down in a brocaded chair, shot his cuffs, and adjusted the creases of his pants as he looked his victim straight in the eye.

"Michael, Michael, Michael," he sighed as if with genuine regret, an emotion made all the more menacing by the dead look in his eyes. "Did it really have to come to this?"

The only answer was the heavy breathing of the man named Michael.

"Tell me," the other continued, glancing down. "Are you going to smoke that cigarette or sniff it?"

Michael looked down at his hand, where he had crushed the unlit cigarette in his fist. Opening his hand, he dumped the crumbled paper and tobacco flakes and, still trembling violently, tried to wipe the residue off with his handkerchief. The small square of cloth slipped from his fingers and fluttered to the ground, where it lay, like a futile flag of surrender.

"Fre . . . Freddie," he stammered. "I can explain. Please. Just give me a chance."

The one named Freddie ignored him, taking a thick cigar from his jacket pocket and lighting it leisurely. "You've got a real good grip there," he said at last through a cloud of thick smoke. "I admire a man who's got a good pair of hands to work with. You're sure no sissy, Michael. I can tell that from just looking at you." He leaned forward in his chair. "Let me take a closer look at those hands of yours, pal."

With an involuntary shudder, Michael quickly concealed his hands behind his back until, at a signal from Freddie, one of the thugs crossed over, yanked one arm in front of him, and half dragged him to where his tormentor was sitting. "Nothing to be afraid of, Mikey boy," purred Freddie. "I just want to read your palm. You know, look into your future, like the fortune-telling lady."

The thug thrust Michael's hand out to Freddie with the sweaty palm up, and the whimpering increased as the helpless and horrified victim watched Freddie produce an elaborate silver-plated switchblade from his pocket. The razor-sharp edge of the blade glinted in the sunlight coming through the windows as Freddie brought its tip close to the quaking flesh of Michael's palm.

"Let's see here," Freddie said with slow deliberation, then nodded as if impressed by what he saw. "Well, well, Mikey boy," he continued. "I've got some good news and some bad news. Which one do you want to hear first?"

Michael tried to form words, but all that came from between his lips was a kind of deep groan.

"Can't hear you, pal," Freddie said, still lightly running the point of the blade around Michael's palm. "You'll have to speak up."

"Pl . . . please," croaked Michael. "A little more time. That's all I'm asking, Freddie."

"I guess we should get the bad news over with first," said

Freddie, ignoring the other's pleas. "That way you've got something to look forward to." He grinned up at his associates. "Sound good to you, boys?" They nodded, and Freddie returned to his examination of Michael's palm. "Now," he continued, "if I remember correctly, this line right here is your life line." He clucked his tongue. "Mikey boy, I hate to break this to you, but it's looking like you're going to have a very, very short life." The knife inched its way toward the base of Michael's trembling thumb.

"Now," Freddie went on, savoring the psychological agony he was putting the other man through, "this line tells me that you're about to star in a new TV program that's like the old sports show, but this one's called *The Wide World of Pain*. And it's coming very soon."

With a lightning quick movement, Freddie had the knife at Michael's throat, holding the point at the exact center of his throbbing jugular. "We don't want that to happen now, do we, pal?" he asked with a vicious hiss. Michael shook his head, careful not to jar the knife at his neck. "Of course, we don't," Freddie said. "And that's where the good news comes in. Are you ready for the good news, Mikey?"

Michael nodded, his eyes wide and tears leaking down his cheeks.

"Good boy," Freddie continued, leaning close and whispering in his ear. "The good news is this: you can avoid that world of hurt and the tragic early death if you listen and listen good." He moved the knifepoint another fraction into the soft flesh of Michael's throat. "Are you listening, Mikey?" Michael answered with another short nod. "That's good," Freddie said, "because here's the good news. You've got until tomorrow to make this all right. You deliver that money by then, and we let you keep your miserable life. That a fair deal?"

"To . . . tomorrow?" Michael stammered. "But how am I going to—"

This time the knife at his neck nicked the skin, drawing a thin rivulet of blood that rolled down onto his collar. "Did I tell you I was psychic?" Freddie asked, still whispering in his ear. "That's right, Mikey. I hear voices. And the voices are saying, 'Don't play around with my boss Mr. Freeman.' They're saying that my employer has better things to do than waste time on your worthless hide. Those voices are saying that tomorrow is the deadline. And I do mean dead."

He grabbed Michael by the hair and viciously yanked his head back. "Do you hear those voices, too, Mikey?" His victim could only stare. "I said," Freddie repeated, "can you hear the voices, Mikey?" He slapped him hard across the mouth, then brought the blade edge fully up against his throat. "Can you?" he screamed. Michael nodded his head for all he was worth. "Good, Mikey," said Freddie, his voice returning to a whisper. "That's real good."

He signaled to his men, and as quickly as they had come, they disappeared, leaving Michael pale and trembling in a pool of his own sweat.

The door to a long black limo opened wide to admit Freddie and the thugs when they exited the revolving door of the hotel. The phone in the backseat rang as they surged into traffic, and the one nearest the console picked it up. He listened for a moment, then handed it to his boss. "It's for you," he said in a voice that sounded as if he had a mouth full of marbles. "It's Mr. Freeman."

Freddie's haughty demeanor changed quickly at the news. Swallowing hard, he took the receiver that was being held out to him. "Freddie here, Mr. Freeman," he said and listened carefully as the voice on the other end began to grill him.

Three miles away, in an office with large windows looking down on a fully equipped, state-of-the-art gym complete with a sparring ring, Sam Freeman paced up and down his plush carpet, chewing on the soggy end of a cigar and shouting into a telephone. All around him were posters and fight cards publicizing some of the biggest and most prestigious matches in the realm of international boxing. The credit above each and every placard was the same: A SAM FREEMAN PRESENTATION.

But at the moment, the legendary fight promoter was in no mood to bask in the past glories of his career. Things weren't going his way, and when things didn't go Sam Freeman's way, somebody, somewhere, was going to have a lot of explaining to do.

"Are you getting soft on me in your old age, Freddie?" Freeman screamed, his bushy white eyebrows rising high on his wrinkled forehead. "Because if you are, I'll get me another enforcer so fast it'll make that tiny little brain of yours spin!"

"No, Mr. Freeman, I swear, this guy is going to pay up. We just need to wait—"

"Wait!" Freeman thundered. "I don't wait for nothing, Freddie. Don't you get that by now? I sent you out on a simple collection job, and you come back telling me I've got to wait! You get that money, you hear me? And don't come back until you do. Understand?"

"I . . . I understand," Freddie murmured on the other end, but Sam Freeman didn't hear him. He had already slammed the receiver back onto its cradle and hurled the soggy stump of his cigar against the window where it landed with a splattering sound and left a dark nicotine stain on the spotless pane.

The limo moved slowly through the clogged downtown traffic, still within sight of the hotel where Freddie and his squad had paid their terrifying visit. In the security office of the same hotel several security guards took a break from filling out routine paperwork to catch a segment of a high-profile press conference unfolding live before the television cameras.

On-screen the heavyweight boxing champion, Antonio Vasquez, fresh from defending his crown, was boasting loudly about his prowess in the ring. Around him, the photographers and reporters captured his every word and movement, eating out of the hand of this larger-than-life sports celebrity.

"You've got to understand," Vasquez was saying in a thickly accented voice. "The power that I have inside me, the power that comes out in my fists of fury"—he held up his hands, still swollen from the night before, as the flashes exploded around him—"the actual source of that power comes from the fact that I am the reincarnation of an ancient Mayan warrior. That warrior never lost a battle, and with him inside me, I am destined to be champ now and for always!"

In the background, the white-haired figure of Sam Freeman stepped forward into the lights, holding up his hands for silence. "The champ will answer a few questions now," he announced, and immediately the room erupted in shouts and waving hands.

At that moment, Orlando, dressed for work at the hotel in his security blazer and tie, entered the room and saw the group of guards gathered around the television. Striding over, he flicked off the screen to the collective groan of the men.

"Come on, you guys," he said. "You can watch that clown on your own time. We've got better things to do around here." He turned to Dexter, who was contentedly munching a bag of corn chips. "You get on up to the top floor, Dex. I want to make sure we've got everything in order for next week."

"But I'm still on my lunch hour," protested Dexter.

"Let me ask you something," Orlando replied. "When isn't it

your lunch hour, Dexter?" Raucous laughter trailed the guard down the hall as he left to follow his orders.

"What are you guys laughing at?" Orlando asked, turning to the others. "You think this place is going to take care of itself?"

The image of the strutting, posturing champion was not being witnessed only in the cramped security center of the hotel. Among the millions upon millions of homes watching the same spectacle at the same moment was a modest apartment in a downtown brownstone not far from a shady park where older people sat on benches and watched the children frolicking in the playground. It was a nice, comfortable neighborhood lined with trees and dotted with mom-and-pop stores and old Italian restaurants, one of the last havens for a quiet life in the ever-increasing noise and chaos of the surrounding city.

On the countertop of a kitchen, which had a window overlooking the park, a small portable television broadcast the same press conference. Alicia stood in the doorway, watching the boastful champ while listening to her friend Kathleen on the phone. In the sink were the remains of a delicious-looking meal—homemade lasagna, garden-fresh salad, and crunchy French bread.

"So," Kathleen was saying, "you have a chance to look over the preacher's manifesto yet?"

Alicia sighed. Sometimes Kathleen was so predictable. "If you mean the brochure from the youth center," she replied, "no, I haven't had time yet. I just finished dinner, and I've got to get Darla to bed. Maybe later tonight if I'm not too tired."

There was a moment of silence on the other end of the line. "This is serious, girl," Kathleen said at last. "I think there might be a cult or something going on there."

"I really don't have time—" Alicia began.

"I tell you what," Kathleen interrupted. "You read that thing tonight, then tomorrow, the two of us will go out and find Darla a new day care."

"Good night, Kathleen," said an exasperated Alicia and, hanging up the phone, she walked down the hall to Darla's bedroom.

Decorated with nursery rhyme figures and artwork she had brought home from the youth center, Darla's room was a sanctuary of innocence that Alicia worked hard to keep that way. Nothing and no one would ever come between her and her precious daughter. As she tucked the little girl into her bed, she couldn't help wondering whether Kathleen was right after all. The last thing Alicia wanted was to expose Darla's tender heart and mind to strange ideas and outmoded myths that would confuse and frighten her. She promised herself she would take a closer look at the center where her daughter spent her days.

"Mommy," Darla asked, looking up from her pillow, the blankets pulled up tight under her chin, "can I say a prayer first?"

"Um . . . sure, honey," replied Alicia, startled at her child's request. Maybe there *was* something fishy going on at that place. "If you really want to."

Darla nodded and, climbing out from beneath the covers, knelt down at her bed, folded her hands, and bowed her head. "Dear heavenly Father," she began with tightly shut eyes, "I pray that You watch out for me and my mommy while we're sleeping. I pray You'd help me to live a good life and to always do what You want me to do. I pray for Geneva and Simon and Orlando."

Opening her eyes, she was about to jump back between the warm sheets when she remembered one more request. Getting back on her knees, she added, "And please help Kathleen not to be such a grouchy person. In Jesus' name, amen."

Alicia hid her smile at the child's last prayer, feeling at the same time a strange tenderness deep in her heart. It was almost as if she could half remember being a child herself and putting her childlike faith into things she couldn't see but knew were real anyway. "That was good, honey," she said softly, stroking Darla's hair. "I know God must have heard you."

"But, Mommy," asked Darla, "if you know that God is listening, why don't you pray?"

For a moment she could find no answer, nothing to tell the little girl about how part of growing up was to stop believing in things you couldn't see and touch and hold. "I . . . don't know," Alicia said finally. "I guess I forgot."

"You can do it now," said the eager child. "I'll teach you!"

Alicia turned away, trying to hide the confusion on her face. "Well, honey," she murmured, "I'm not sure I really have very much to say to God."

"Orlando says that it doesn't matter," Darla replied. "Orlando says that even if we don't have anything to say to God, He always has something to say to us."

"He says that, does he?" Alicia responded, turning back to her child. "Well, that's wonderful for Orlando. But you can't always believe everything people say to you, Darla. Sometimes, they might not know what's best for you."

Darla thought for a moment, her high forehead wrinkling with the effort. "Well," she said at last, "if Orlando is right, then what do you think God would want to say to you, Mommy?"

Alicia swallowed hard, feeling a sharp pang of emotion without knowing exactly why or where it had come from. "I wish I knew, honey," she said at last. "I wish I knew."

Later that evening Alicia sat alone in a pool of light from a living room reading lamp. In her hands she held the pamphlet for the youth center that Kathleen had given her. She lingered for a long time over the photo of a smiling child on the cover under-neath a headline that read "The Power to Heal Our Nation."

Turning the brochure over, she found herself suddenly face-to-face with a photo of Orlando Leone, his handsome face spark-ing a strange, faint attraction within her.

"Well, hello, Mr. Orlando Leone," she said and, opening the pamphlet, read the following words printed boldly on the inside cover.

"'The joy of the Lord is my strength.' Those simple words were written thousands of years ago, and yet here, in our city, those same words are changing lives forever. It's my mission, my calling in life, to help children of all ages to find the joy through studying God's Word and through teaching them the difference between right and wrong in a world that too often blurs the distinctions. I'm here, along with my dedicated staff, to make a difference."

It was signed *Orlando Leone*.

For a long moment Alicia sat silent and still while the words on the page echoed in her mind. *The joy of the Lord is my strength.* She wondered what that meant exactly, but at the same time, she had the feeling that she already knew and that the truth of those words had been planted in her life from as long ago as she could remember, when she was Darla's age or maybe even younger.

Without really knowing why, she rose from her chair and made her way down the hall to her small sculpting studio. There, with the sounds of traffic and the barking of a lonely dog to keep her company, she began sketching out the design for a new work that, for the moment, was left untitled.

CHAPTER FIVE

THE SUN SHONE THROUGH THE BLINDS DIRECTLY ONTO Orlando's face as he lay in the deep sleep of the truly exhausted on the threadbare cushions of the couch in his office. Even with the bright light blazing on his lids, Orlando might well have continued his dreamless slumber if it had not been for the persistent ring of a telephone that slowly roused him from sleep like a man emerging from a deep, dark tunnel.

No more than half conscious, he stumbled across the office to the phone on the desk and picked up the receiver. "Hello?" he mumbled, his mind still foggy and his voice indistinct.

A loud voice greeted him from the other end of the line. "Orlando!" shouted his attorney and childhood friend Pete. "Time to rise and shine."

"Pete," Orlando groaned. "I should have known it'd be you." Then sudden trepidation brought him fully awake. "Don't tell me I missed another meeting," he lamented.

"No," Pete reassured him. "You didn't miss a thing." In the background behind Pete, Orlando could hear the unmistakable sounds of a busy gym: skipping rope, a punching bag being pummeled, and the all-too-familiar sound of a ringside bell.

"Where are you?" he asked his friend.

"That's what I'm trying to tell you," Pete shouted to make himself heard over the noise. "Listen, I'm down here at Shiller's Gym, and there's somebody here I think you need to check out right away."

"Come on, Pete," replied Orlando, trying to contain his annoyance. The guy was always trying to lure him back into the boxing ring, just to watch Orlando's artistry within the ropes. Any reason would do.

"No, no, no," Pete insisted. "This is different, Orlando! They've got a kid down here, a real contender. He won an Olympic gold. His name's Erik West. You must have heard of him."

"Sure, I've heard of him," Orlando conceded, "but look, I've got a million things to do around here and I can't just—"

"But this kid's your number one fan," Pete interrupted. "He's had ten pro bouts, and he's telling me he's watched you since *you* were on the Olympic team. He has studied how you worked to get himself ready for each of his fights. He knows more stats about you than I do. C'mon, Champ. He knows you work out down here. Could you please come down and go a few rounds with him? Just to see what he's got. What do you say? It'll be a thrill for him. You're his idol."

"What has this got to do with you?" Orlando asked suspiciously.

"Well, if you've got to know, the kid's got a few trouble spots," answered the chagrined lawyer, "and I owe his manager a favor. Come on, do this for me, and we'll call it even for all that free legal work I did for your project."

Orlando heaved a sigh. "Look," he said finally, "I don't mind going a round or two with this guy, but you know I'm not into fighting any gym wars. I've got responsibilities. I can't run the risk of anybody getting their head cracked open— especially me."

"No one's going to get hurt," insisted Pete. "You're the man, Orlando."

After hanging up, Orlando just shook his head. *Most fans just want an autograph from their favorite stars,* he thought ruefully. *Mine want to punch me in the face. What did I do to deserve this?*

A half hour later, Orlando arrived at the gym, a place he had been familiar with ever since his preteen days when he wasn't much more than just another kid looking to make his way in the most treacherous and unforgiving sport there is. The old place hadn't changed much since then: old fight bills were still peeling off the walls, the heavy smell of sweat hung in the air, and the sounds of men pushing their bodies to the limit sent noisy echoes off the walls.

Orlando had been coming regularly to this place, even after he had quit the ring, and he was a welcome arrival every time he pushed through the door with his workout clothes in an old canvas duffel bag. The old-timers knew him best, and they invariably stopped whatever they were doing to greet him when he came for his weekly routine.

"Orlando!" cried one trainer, working with his young heavyweight "bolo" protégé on the heavy bag. "Looking good, my man!"

"Hey, Brady," replied Orlando as he scanned the crowded room for some sign of Pete. "They still have you on the payroll?"

"They couldn't keep me away," the grizzled older man replied. "I'd torture these young mutts for free if I had to." He turned to the young boxer and pointed with pride to Orlando. "See that guy?" he demanded. "When Antonio Vasquez, the heavyweight champ of the world, was nothing more than a kid whose feet were too big for him, Orlando here used to come upside his head on a regular basis . . . right here in this very gym."

"No kidding," said the kid, genuinely impressed.

"Hey," said Brady, "what are you doing standing around with your jaw hanging open? Get back on the bag, you lazy good-for-nothing."

Orlando laughed. "Don't pay any attention to Brady, kid," he told the young fighter. "They say he got knocked in the head once too often when he was a referee."

Crossing the room, Orlando finally spotted Pete behind the ropes of the sparring ring, deep in conversation with a silver-haired gentleman in a well-tailored suit. Next to him was a bright-eyed young man in boxing trunks and gloves who looked over in awe as Orlando approached. Orlando recognized him at once from television coverage of the Olympic Games—he was Erik West, one of the most promising young heavyweight fighters on the circuit.

"Orlando," Pete cried as he saw his friend approaching. "I knew you'd make it. I told these guys." He turned to the others. "Didn't I tell you? My pal Orlando Leone never lets you down."

He stood to one side as he made introductions all around. "Orlando," he said, gesturing to the silver-haired man, "I want you to meet a very important individual. This is Marco Shavarone of the German Boxing League. And this," he said proudly, putting his arm around the young fighter, "is the one and only Erik West, the next heavyweight champion of the world."

Orlando shook hands with the two, letting Erik hold on for an extra moment as he pumped away and grinned like a kid at Christmas. "Orlando Leone," he said, savoring the name. "I'm so honored to meet you. I think I must be your biggest fan. I watched all your fights on video and followed every move. You're brilliant."

Orlando wondered briefly if the fresh-faced kid had watched

the video of his very last fight—if he had seen the man lying pale and motionless on the bloodstained canvas—but instead of asking, he just smiled and nodded. "It's a pleasure to meet you too," he said. "I hear you're quite a fighter."

Erik blushed at the compliment from his idol, even as Pete began talking in his usual fast and furious manner. "Marco here represents Erik, and I was just telling them how you'd agreed to rock and roll with the kid for a couple of rounds. You know, maybe give him a few pointers."

Orlando turned to Marco Shavarone. "Okay. Let's talk about the other reason I'm here, other than to be a veteran sparring partner. Anything you're looking for in particular?" he asked.

"Erik's been getting tagged with a lot of overhand rights," said the manager with a thick German accent. "He also seems to be having some trouble getting off the ropes. We thought perhaps a man of your expertise might be able to help pinpoint some of these problems and suggest solutions." He bowed slightly at the waist. "I would be very much in your debt if you might agree to perform this service."

"No problem," replied Orlando with a quick look at his lawyer. "Any friend of Pete's is a friend of mine."

He turned to Erik. "Tell you what," he said, clapping the fighter on the back. "Let's just have a little fun with it. Go a few rounds and get a feel for what's happening up there." He laughed. "Give me what you've got, kid, but remember . . . I'm a few years older than you are. So let's keep it slick and to the point, okay? You ready?" he said as he pulled up the ropes, "step into my office."

"Sure thing, Mr. Leone," Erik said. Orlando headed to the locker room where he quickly dressed out. When he returned, the two men climbed into the ring.

For the next several minutes, Orlando put Erik through his paces, running a variety of combinations on him, probing for his weak spots, and giving him plenty of chances to make a move when the opportunity presented itself. At first, the young fighter was obviously holding back, out of respect for the veteran fighter, but after a few accurately placed hits with Orlando's famed overhand right, Erik began to open up and concentrate on fighting his best fight. It was a task that proved easier said than done. Orlando, for all the age difference between them, proved to be a very elusive target, bobbing and weaving, ducking and dancing, until the kid started swinging wildly in hopes of connecting. When the bell rang at the end of the round, both men were covered in sweat.

"So?" said Pete as Orlando, panting heavily, wiped his face dry. "What's the story?"

Orlando turned to Shavarone and, although reluctant to lay it all on the line, knew that it was now or never as far as correcting Erik's mistakes was concerned. "First of all," he explained, "he's got to work on his hand movement. He appears very slow for a guy of his size and weight. Second, and even more important, he has a habit of shifting his shoulders before he punches. I see everything a second before it lands. Plus, he's got a bad habit of straightening his back just before he jabs. He's telegraphing every move. As soon as I see that right shoulder start to rise, I know it's time to unload my right. And I connect every time." He shrugged. "I was going easy on him. When he gets higher in the pro ranks, you better believe some young lion will decapitate him."

"That's exactly what I've been telling him!" exclaimed Shavarone. "Please, Mr. Leone, would you agree to go a few more rounds with my client and show him what he must do?"

"If I was ten years younger, it'd be no big deal," Orlando had to confess. "But the truth is, that round got me pretty winded."

He looked across the gym to where Brady was still working with the young fighter at the punching bag. "Tell you what I will do, though," he said and called out to the trainer. "Brady, pull me out your best heavyweight for five or six rounds. Then give me 'bolo.'"

For the next half hour, using Brady's protégé as Erik's sparring partner, he coached the former Olympic star with an intensity and focus that seemed to be a natural-born trait, a gut-level understanding of the tactics and strategy of boxing that was something no one could ever have taught him. Yet it was a mark of Orlando's remarkable skill at communicating, combined with his innate love of the game, that by the end of six practice rounds, Erik West was routinely deflecting his opponent's overhand right, even as he had learned to keep his shoulder low and his intentions to himself.

It was now Shavarone's turn to pump Orlando's hand enthusiastically. "I can't thank you enough, Mr. Leone," he said. "You've done wonders for the boy and in such a short time! You really should be a coach, you know."

Orlando accepted the compliment, but shook his head. "I appreciate it, Mr. Shavarone," he said. "But it's not my game anymore. I've got other fights that take up my time these days." As the manager, his client, and Pete watched with silent admiration, Orlando silently turned and headed for the showers.

Across town a very different activity had captured the attention of Alicia as she worked intently with a group of college students in a sculpture class that took place in a large, airy studio loft in the downtown arts district. Just finishing up with a few pointers to one of her more promising pupils, she noticed for the first time in what seemed like hours that the class time had long since been over. So engrossed was everyone in the process of bringing stone and clay to life that none of them had noticed.

"Okay, everyone," she announced. "That's it for today. I'll see you next week." Then she also noticed for the first time that Kathleen was standing in the classroom doorway. "Hey," she said as she gathered her jacket and purse from her desk.

"You sure do love playing with that stuff," Kathleen marveled. "Look at your hands, girl. Looks like you've been eating mud."

Alicia laughed. "I'll wash up and be right with you."

As she waited for her friend, Kathleen spotted Darla in one corner of the spacious loft, carefully molding her own figures out of modeling clay. Crossing to the little girl, she knelt down. "Hey, wonder girl," she said, kissing her on the top of the head, "what are you working on so hard there?"

Darla held up two small figures, childishly shaped but still recognizably human. "This one is Jesus," she said proudly. "And this is the man who was lame." She set them carefully on the floor next to each other. "See, Kathleen," she explained. "Jesus is going to heal the man who can't walk."

Kathleen bit her lower lip and nodded. Then hurrying away, she spotted Alicia coming out of the washroom and grabbed her by the arm. "There you are!" she said, her eyes wide.

"What on the earth is the matter with you?" Alicia asked, startled by her friend's alarmed expression.

In answer, Kathleen nodded across the room in the direction of Darla. "It's worse than I thought," she said in a hoarse whisper.

"What's worse?" demanded a frustrated Alicia. Sometimes Kathleen could be so dramatic. "What are you talking about?"

"Exhibit A," replied Kathleen vehemently. "Darla is making a little clay Jesus, who is going to heal a little clay disabled man." She glared at Alicia. "What's next, girlfriend? A little bald Darla in an orange robe, handing out tracts at the airport?"

Alicia sighed. "I appreciate your concern," she said, laying a hand on Kathleen's arm. "Really I do. Believe me, I've thought about what you've said. But, well, maybe it isn't such a big deal after all." She smiled encouragingly. "I mean, my parents took me to Sunday school when I was Darla's age, and I didn't turn out so bad, did I? Would you feel better if Jesus was mugging the crippled man?"

Kathleen looked at her through narrowed eyes. "What's that got to do with it?" she demanded. "It's not the same thing at all."

"Listen," Alicia continued, trying her best to explain feelings she hadn't quite put a name to, "I just want my little girl to be happy. That's all. If all this Jesus stuff helps her to feel secure, what harm is there in that?"

"I'll tell you what harm there is!" Kathleen shot back. "It's all a bunch of fairy tales they're feeding those innocent little minds. Darla needs to know what the real world is all about."

"There's plenty of time for her to find that out," Alicia countered. "Besides, I think she's getting a lot of good input at the youth center. In fact . . ." She hesitated.

"In fact, what?" probed the suddenly suspicious Kathleen.

Alicia swallowed hard. "I promised Darla I'd go with her to the youth service tonight. I want to talk to that Mr. Leone anyway. About the job."

Kathleen sniffed haughtily. "You do what you want, girl," she said with a frosty air. "You just remember this when you and your little girl are caught up in all that religious mumbo jumbo." She leaned in close. "They're hypocrites, Alicia. Every last one of them. They'll be pouring sugar in your ear while they've got a hand in your pocket. You mark my words."

CHAPTER SIX

KATHLEEN'S WORDS WERE STILL ECHOING IN ALICIA'S EARS later that evening when she and Darla arrived at the youth center amid a crowd of happy and excited participants for the evening service. Entering the main hall, they could hear music and shouts of pure joy echoing down the hall as the assembly joined in with the gospel choir to sing a rousing song of praise, with an authentic Latin percussion section backed by a pumping bass, drums, guitar, and electric piano. Up onstage in front of the crowd, the pastor named Simon banged on a tambourine in time to the music and urged the gathering on to greater and greater expressions of love, passion for God, and devotion. Sweat poured from his wrinkled skin, soaking his clerical collar, and he was barely able to get out the words to the songs through his panting breath, but the beaming smile on his face spoke more loudly of his spiritual strength than of any physical limitation.

The music roared to a conclusion, and as the standing-room-only crowd clapped and shouted out words of exaltation and encouragement, Orlando ran down the aisle and jumped onto the stage with all the grace and agility of a man half his age. Alicia, who had let Darla run off to join her friends as soon as they entered the building, watched Orlando carefully from the back of the room: the feeling she had had about him ever since first laying eyes on his picture grew stronger in the ecstatic jubilation of the room. Orlando seemed bathed in a bright light all his own, and the happiness and celebration going on all around him seemed to feed his spirit like a hungry child sitting down at a feast.

"All right!" he shouted as the crowd roared its approval. He turned around and clapped the beaming black man on the back. "Thank you, Elder Simon." Then raising his hands, he sent up a joyful expression of thanksgiving that soon had the whole crowd joining in. "And thank You, Jesus! Thank You, Lord!" he exclaimed as the assembly echoed his words.

The tumult lasted for several minutes before the people settled down enough for Orlando to continue. Once they had taken their seats and turned their attention to him, he slipped the microphone off the stand and began to pace the stage, as if he could barely contain the energy and enthusiasm he felt.

"Some folks might tell you that we're getting entirely too rowdy and out of control around here when it comes to expressing our faith," he began. The attention of his congregation was so intense a pin could have been heard dropping on the street outside. "But when I hear that kind of talk, I always wonder, How else do they expect delivered people to act?" A fresh round of cheering ensued as Orlando raised his hands as a way of giving all the glory back to God.

"The Bible says that the joy of the Lord is our strength," he continued after the noise had subsided. "Which means that if you ain't got no joy, then you ain't got no strength. Right?" Shouts of "Right on!" and "Preach it!" could be heard around the hall. "I have a question for each and every one of you here tonight," Orlando continued over the cries. "The question is this: How many of you want to be joyous, happy, and strong Christians?"

Once again the hall erupted in pandemonium, this time with the band striking up another gospel tune. The congregation sang along as Orlando held out the microphone to them, and it was a good five minutes before he could restore enough order to continue his message.

"Lots of people talk about how they are discouraged coming to church because of all the hypocrisy they see around them," he said at last as the murmuring crowd settled down. "Seems like every time they come through the doors of the Lord's house, all they can find is people who are lying and stealing, cheating on their wives, and getting drunk on Saturday night."

The people began to mutter among themselves, not exactly sure where their pastor was going with his sermon. From the back of the room, Alicia found herself nodding in agreement. "You've sure got that right," she said under her breath as Orlando continued.

"But there's a flip side to that particular very popular shiny silver dollar," he was saying. "There's a very good reason why certain individuals can truthfully say that they've found all those human failings inside a church." He paused, looking around the room as if he were half expecting someone to shout out the answer. "The reason is the same one," he continued, "that explains why I can stand in an airport and, ninety-nine times out of a hundred, spot anybody Italian and anyone who's a boxer."

His voice dropped, and suddenly the large room felt small and intimate, as if Orlando were having a personal conversation with each and every member of the congregation. "The reason," he explained, "is that all my life I've been an Italian, and I've been a prizefighter. Let me tell you something, people!" he exclaimed, his voice rising again. "You're always going to identify with the very thing that you know most about."

Once again the hall was silent as the crowd waited breathlessly for Orlando's next words. "Let me repeat that," he said at last. "You're always going to identify with the very thing that you're most familiar with. It's just human nature."

"Amen," shouted a voice from the side, and several others joined in the refrain. From her place in the back, Alicia felt her mind racing, trying to comprehend exactly what Orlando was saying and what it might mean to her.

"If there is lying or stealing, cheating or drunkenness in your heart," Orlando explained, "you can bet your life that's going to be your main point of identification." He leaned forward off the edge of the stage as though he wanted to reach out and touch each individual with his words. "See, people," he said, "what we're trying to do here is to change hearts. You change a person's heart, and that means you change what he identifies with." He held up his finger to make his next point. "If you remember one thing I say tonight, remember this: church was never meant to be a sanctuary for saints. It was meant to be a hospital for sinners."

More shouts of "Amen!" resounded through the hall joined by stomps and whistles. But the crowd quieted quickly when Orlando raised his hand to still them. There was more to come. "Now," he said, "it's also true that some of you out there tonight might need a little bit more than just a visit to the hospital. You might be needing some time in intensive care."

While a good portion of the crowd laughed at the remark, there were others who seemed to be hanging on his every word. "But that's what God has been doing for thousands of years and what I want to see done here tonight. I want to follow His guidance and make a place where people with broken lives, broken hearts, and broken minds can come and find healing."

His voice was loud and clear now, its strength reaching to the far corners of the hall. "I want to build a place where young people can come and discover God's will for their lives, His personal destiny for each and every one of them. I want to provide a place where they can find shelter from the storms of the world, a place where they can avoid the snares and temptations that await them around every corner out there."

Several people were standing now, their arms outstretched, thanking God for the words of truth being spoken. Orlando raised his arms, too, and for a long moment seemed lost in silent prayer. Alicia watched carefully, telling herself that if this was all an act, then Orlando Leone deserved an Academy Award. The tingling warmth she felt deep in her spirit was real enough. So, also, was the sudden and overwhelming conviction that his words were meant for her as much as anyone sitting near her.

At last Orlando seemed to return to the reality of the youth center and began talking again, even as he gestured offstage. "Young people are what this place is all about," he was saying. "It's why God has blessed our work here and why He's going to continue to be in our corner for every fight that comes along." To Alicia's dumbfounded surprise, a small and familiar figure walked into the spotlight from the edge of the stage. It was Darla. "Here's one of those reasons now," Orlando announced. "Her name is Darla, and she's going to sing a song for us tonight. Now I want you all to listen carefully to the words she's going to sing. Especially those of you in the workplace who do battle on the front lines."

Alicia had had no idea that her daughter was going to sing this evening, but suddenly she understood why Darla had been so insistent on her mother attending. It was going to be a surprise, and Alicia felt tears flood her eyes at the thought of her little girl wanting to make this moment special for her mother. As Geneva sat at the keyboards and began to play the soft and tender chords of "'Tis So Sweet," the choir on the risers joined in with heavenly harmony, and Darla's clear, bright voice filled the room like the breath of a soulful little angel. The tears in Alicia's eyes now flowed freely down her cheeks, and her pounding heart felt as if it were rising in her throat. *What's happening to me,* she wondered as the words of the song penetrated deep into her spirit, *and what is this presence that I feel all around me?*

As Darla concluded the final verse, the choir joined in and helped her finish the final chorus. Then Geneva kept playing quietly, and Orlando stepped back up, taking the microphone from the child's hands. "We're going to open up the altars right now," he said in a low voice, "just as we do every night for people out there who want to ask the Lord to come into their hearts and make their lives new. If you feel a special call inside you right now, that's because this is your moment of truth. Don't let it slip by you because you are afraid of what someone might think. The Lord is calling some of you tonight. He's reaching out to take you by the hand."

From the side of the stage, Darla watched as her mother walked slowly but deliberately down the aisle toward her, her face wet with tears and a brilliant light burning in her eyes.

Thank You, Lord, the young child said in silent prayer as Alicia stood at the foot of the altar. *Thank You for saving my mommy.*

CHAPTER SEVEN

A SCREAM OF AGONY ECHOED DOWN THE FILTHY, RAT-infested back alley in one of the city's most run-down and neglected neighborhoods. The bums and drunks and streetwalkers who heard the bloodcurdling sound ducked their heads and picked up their shambling pace. The last thing anyone wanted in this place was to be part of someone else's trouble.

Six stories above the alleyway a man screamed again, pleading desperately for his life. A pair of strong hands held him dangling from the open window of a fleabag hotel. A flickering neon sign lit the lurid scene, and the man's strangled cries sent frightened pigeons fluttering up from their roosts under the eaves of the hotel roof.

Sitting on the stained, sprung mattress in the dim and dirty room, Freddie smoked a cigarette as he grimly watched his two muscle-bound cronies work over Michael. As one held him under the arms out the window, the other grabbed him by the hair and repeatedly banged his head against the hotel's brick wall.

"I asked you a simple question," the thug was saying. "You got Mr. Freeman's money or don't you?"

"I'll get the money!" Michael sobbed in pain and terror. "I swear. Just give me a little more time, I'm begging you!"

"That's not the answer we want to hear," said his associate. "Freddie here already gave you another day, you scumbag. You got as much time as you're going to get."

"I'm working on it, Freddie. You . . . you've got to believe me," Michael stammered, trying to peer over the sill at his tormentor. "Look, what good am I to you dead, Freddie? A corpse can't give Mr. Freeman back his money."

Freddie dropped the cigarette on the carpet and sighed. "The question isn't, What good are you to me dead?" he said with utter contempt. "Mikey boy, the question is, What good are you to me alive?" He nodded to his enforcers, and with no more thought than they would give to crushing a cockroach, they let Michael drop. His scream came to an abrupt end as his body crashed through a tree, smashed a small bush, and slammed against the concrete alley, its echo fading into the sounds of passing traffic and the loud rock and roll coming from a barroom jukebox down the street.

Three minutes later the threesome emerged from the battered front door of the hotel and hurried across the street to where a waiting limo idled. As the thugs climbed into the front seats, Freddie took his place in the back, where two familiar figures waited. One was Sam Freeman, wearing an ominous frown on his face. The other was Antonio Vasquez, the heavyweight champion of the world, drinking deeply from a bottle of champagne in his ham hock–sized fist as he listened to a Walkman clamped over his ears.

"You solve our little problem?" Freeman asked his flunky as the limousine pulled away and onto the main boulevard heading uptown.

"Not the way we had hoped. But it's solved," said Freddie, not daring to look his boss in the eye.

Freeman turned to stare out the window at the burned-out building and shuttered storefront passing by. "I'm disappointed,

Freddie," he said. "I am not the kind of man who enjoys losing out on his investments."

"Mr. Freeman," Freddie replied firmly but without feeling, "you hired me to tell your loose ends to pay or else. Well, I'm your 'or else.' I did my job. I made that guy an example to others who ever try to rip you off. They're not going to forget what can happen if they don't make good on their obligations, sir. I make sure people always know you mean business."

Freeman turned and stared at Freddie and smiled. He knew that Freddie was his man, but also a violent, loose cannon who had to be handled carefully.

Then as if he had dropped one mask and picked up another to cover his true nature, Freeman turned smiling to Vasquez, who looked completely oblivious to the menacing conversation that had just concluded. "So, Champ," he said with fatherly concern. "You hungry? Where would you like to eat?"

Clearly irritated at the intrusion, Vasquez lifted the headphones of his Walkman. "You've got to ask?" he said in a peeved tone of voice. "La Chareada's, of course."

"Sure thing, Champ," replied Freeman as Vasquez returned to the blaring rap music inside the headphones. Freeman rolled his eyes, muttering to himself, "Mexican again? Doesn't this guy ever get tired of burritos?" He leaned forward to the driver. "La Chareada's," he ordered.

"Sure thing," said the thug behind the wheel, stepping on the accelerator.

Freeman turned to Freddie. "You," he said and pointed at the car phone. "Call up Goldblatt's. Tell them to deliver some matzo ball soup and chopped chicken liver to La Chareada's." He sighed. "I've got to have some real food every once in a while. I'm only human, ain't I?" He stared at Freddie, who looked as if he wasn't quite sure of the answer. "I said," repeated Freeman, "I'm only human, ain't I?"

"Absolutely, Mr. Freeman," Freddie replied quickly. "I'm only human. I'll take a cheese steak sandwich."

The limo sped by a city block where, under the light of a street lamp, a group of people had gathered to talk happily and excitedly among themselves. As its taillights disappeared around a corner, Alicia and Darla emerged onto the front steps of the youth center. Alicia bent down to give her daughter a warm and affectionate hug.

"You were wonderful tonight, honey," she said, her heart about to burst with love and gratitude for the blessing that the little girl had brought to her life.

"Were you surprised, Mommy?" Darla asked excitedly.

"More than you'll ever know, sweetheart," was Alicia's heartfelt reply.

"She's been planning that all week," said a voice behind them.

Rising, Alicia turned to face Orlando Leone. A long moment passed as the two simply looked at each other, their eyes locked, an electric surge of mutual attraction passing between them.

"This is my mommy," said Darla at last with a hint of impatience.

"Nice to meet you, Mrs. Corbin," Orlando said softly, sticking out his hand without taking his eyes off her.

"It's Miss Corbin," she replied, her hand trembling slightly as it touched his hand for the first time. "But, please, you can call me Alicia."

"You can call him Orlando," piped up Darla, tugging at her mother's dress.

Orlando smiled. "Yes," he said, finally breaking eye contact to smile down at Darla. "Please do."

"It's a pleasure to meet you finally," Alicia said, the spell of their first encounter broken for the moment. "I've . . . heard a lot about you."

"Oh," replied Orlando with a bashful grin, "don't believe everything you hear."

"Seriously," Alicia pressed, wanting suddenly to tell him of her evening's experience, "I really want to thank you for what you said up there tonight. I think it was something I've been needing to hear for a long time."

"Well," answered Orlando, still grinning foolishly, "we aim to please. I guess you could call us a one-stop shopping center for all your spiritual needs."

"I have to admit," Alicia continued, "at first I wasn't so sure . . . I mean, about Darla getting exposed to all that . . . religion. But I'm glad now. I can see you really have her best interests at heart."

Orlando nodded, putting his hand on the little girl's head. "She's one of my favorite kids around here," he said. "Everyone just naturally takes to her. She owns a piece of my heart, and she knows it."

A moment of awkward silence followed, and when they spoke again, they stumbled over each other's words.

Orlando smiled. "Please," he said. "Go ahead."

"I was going to say," responded Alicia, "that it would probably be good for us to meet again." Realizing the implications of her words, she blushed. "I . . . I mean," she stammered, "to talk about the sculpture you want. I'm not really sure what you have in mind."

"To be honest," Orlando said, "I'm not really sure I can afford an artist of your caliber. I looked at your brochure. It was very impressive."

"It's something I really love doing," Alicia admitted.

"It shows," Orlando assured her. "But the fact is, we're kind of stretched to the limit around here, financially speaking and in just about every other way, too, I guess. We really need a bigger facility with more activities for the kids."

"Why don't you tell me what you have in mind," Alicia suggested. "Then we can figure out what it might cost."

"Well," Orlando answered, "what I really need is something for my investors to connect with. You know, some kind of symbol that would represent what I'm trying to do."

"And what are you trying to do?" queried Alicia.

Orlando began to answer, then had another idea. "It's kind of a long story," he said. "Maybe, if it's all right with you, I could drop by sometime soon and explain it all to you."

"Good idea," replied Alicia before adding, just a little too quickly, "when and where?"

On her way home, Alicia pondered everything that had happened. To her surprise, her thoughts kept returning to Orlando. Of course, his muscular build, his thick curly hair, and the confidence with which he carried himself would have attracted the attention of most women, not to mention a single mother who'd been without a romantic interest in her life for a little too long. But it wasn't his obvious assets that drew Alicia to Orlando. She could sense there was something different about this guy— the way the kids at the center gathered around him, the love for Darla that Alicia could see in his eyes. Something about the way he took in life radiated joy and a sense of purpose.

It was a beautiful early autumn afternoon two days later when Orlando stood on the stoop of Alicia's apartment building, took a deep breath of the crisp air, and rang the doorbell. She answered the door a moment later, dressed in casual work clothes, her hands darkly smudged with charcoal from a day spent at the artist's easel.

Once again the second hand of her wristwatch seemed to

slow as they looked at each other, pleasantries falling away as the look that passed between them sent a message no words could describe. Finally Alicia laughed and stood aside for him to enter.

"My goodness," she remarked. "Please excuse my appearance. I've been working all afternoon. I guess I lost track of time."

"I think you look great," commented Orlando, who was carrying a manila envelope under his arm. "It's always good to see people," he added, hesitating for a moment, "as they really are."

Alicia led him into the apartment and through the hall to her studio where various sketches and drawings of projects old and new hung on the walls. Orlando gave out a low whistle. "Quite a setup you've got here," he remarked, obviously impressed.

"Yes," replied Alicia as she hurried across the room to turn her easel to the wall. She sneaked a glance at the unfinished likeness of Orlando that she had been working on when he arrived. *It doesn't quite capture the special light in his eyes,* she thought. "I've been very fortunate. I teach classes downstairs, and the school that hired me lets us live in this apartment rent free."

"Now that's what I call a blessing," remarked Orlando. "God must be looking out for you."

"Yes," replied Alicia as if the thought had just occurred to her. "I guess you're right." She offered him a chair. "So," she said as they took their places at a worktable, "have you ever commissioned a piece of sculpture before?"

Orlando smiled. "The only time I ever got involved in sculpture," he admitted, "was when I was a kid. I was at a church picnic, and I carved a statue of Yogi Bear out of a watermelon."

Alicia laughed. "What happened to it?" she asked.

"The other kids ate it," Orlando replied with a shrug.

"That must have been traumatic," commented Alicia with a teasing glint in her eye.

"You know," answered Orlando, "some nights I still wake up screaming."

This time they both laughed. *It's like bells ringing,* thought Orlando as he listened to her. Her laugh was as beautiful as her voice. He cleared his throat, not wanting to get caught up in another of their awkward silences. Picking up the manila envelope he had set on the table, he opened its clasp and took out a pile of photographs. "I thought these might help," he said.

Curious, Alicia began looking through them. Most were old and faded black-and-white shots of a loving couple in 1950s-style clothing. In a few others, a small child was between them, smiling broadly into the camera as he held his parents' hands. The resemblance was too close to miss. Alicia knew she was looking at Orlando as a young boy.

"Alicia," he said proudly, "meet the family. Family, meet Alicia."

Alicia grinned. "Pleased to meet you," she replied, bowing slightly at the heap of photos. "So," she added, "who exactly are my new friends?"

Orlando pointed to a photo of a young Geneva. "This is my mom, Geneva," he explained. "She kind of raised me single-handedly after my dad died. Always made sure I went to church, and when you meet my mother, you'll understand why I never refused." He turned to her. "She was at the service the other day. The woman in the jogging suit. You might have seen her. She's a real spitfire!"

"I absolutely remember her. But I would have never guessed she was your mother," Alicia replied, recalling a bustling woman who seemed to be everywhere at once. On another photo she pointed to a man next to Orlando's mother. "And this is your father?" she asked.

"Sure is," answered Orlando. "Mom says she can really see him in me sometimes. Can you?"

She looked from the photo to Orlando and back again. "Well, if you take away the mustache and the glasses, you guys could be twins," she affirmed, then in a softer voice asked, "How did he die?"

A dark cloud of memory passed suddenly over Orlando's face. "He was walking home one night with the Sunday offering," he recounted in a low voice. "He crossed paths with a couple of gangbangers. They took him out—four shots, point-blank range. And all for eight hundred and fourteen dollars."

"I'm so sorry, Orlando," she said, and he immediately knew that the empathy and compassion in her voice were authentic. She reached out to touch his hand, and for a moment all he could focus on was the gentle touch of her fingers.

"I used to be mad at God for what happened," he said at last. "But I finally understood that His ways are different from ours. See, my dad was a construction worker before he got the call to preach the Word. He quit his job and started a small street mission outreach. We just kept adding on until we got the building we have now."

"You mean the youth center?" asked Alicia.

Orlando nodded. "In the old days, he'd bring kids in by playing the accordion on the street. He was pretty good too. After he was killed, I wondered what was going to happen to all the hard work he'd done to build that place up." He smiled and shrugged. "Eventually, years later, I realized God wanted me to pick up where he'd left off. But I couldn't just walk away from my boxing career because by then it was in full swing. I had a title fight coming up. So I was kind of stuck. Looking back, I can see now how maybe his dying was just a way for me to begin really living my life out for its real purpose."

Alicia returned to the photos. "Who's this?" she asked when she came across a snapshot of a handsome young man who also had a passing resemblance to Orlando.

"Oh, that's my brother, Alfredo," he explained. "He's eight years older. We were . . . close once," he added, troubled again by the memories evoked by her questions.

"What happened to him?" Alicia couldn't help asking.

"It's a long story." Orlando seemed unwilling to say more.

"I've got time," Alicia gently prodded. She rose and walked to a small hot plate on a stand near the table. Filling a kettle with water from a cooler, she took down two cups and dropped a tea bag in each. "That is," she said as she prepared the drinks, "if you want to tell me."

To Orlando's surprise, he discovered that he very much did want to tell this beautiful and sympathetic woman. Suddenly he wanted her to know everything about him.

"When my father was killed," he began, "Alfredo blamed God, just like I did. Only he was sixteen and a lot more strong-willed. He stopped going to church and kept his distance from the family. Actually," he continued, casting his mind back to those dark days, "he got himself another family . . . a gang family. Within a few years he was a real hard-core street hood. My mother forbade me to have anything whatsoever to do with him, but he was my brother, after all, and the only male figure in my life that I could look up to. I loved him and admired him. I respected his utter fearlessness even though he was a gangbanger."

The kettle began to whistle, and Alicia, turning off the hot plate, poured the hot water into the cups. "Go on," she urged him.

"I idolized him," Orlando admitted. "He was my hero. After all, I was really too young to remember much about my dad. I would do anything I could to get Alfredo's respect, and since I knew that what he respected more than anything was a tough guy, I tried to be one. So I decided to enroll in a boxing program at the YMCA." He sighed deeply, obviously still pained by the recollections. "Boxing did the trick," he continued. "I had Alfredo's respect and admiration. Even more important, when I started getting good, he was always at my matches. He'd bring his friends to watch me. Eventually, many years later, he became my manager. It was like a dream come true. I was happy just to be around him. Even my mother didn't stand in the way. I think deep down in her heart she knew I needed a man to be part of my life, even if that man had a police record as long as your arm."

"Did he actually become your manager?" Alicia asked as she set down the teacups on the table.

"He sure did," Orlando stated. "And I sometimes think I stayed in the game just to keep close to him. But then . . . well, let's just say something happened that made me want to get out of boxing in the worst way."

"What happened?" Alicia queried, concerned to see a troubled look clouding Orlando's eyes.

"That's another story," he replied. "But once I quit the ring, my brother wouldn't have anything else to do with me. He took it like a personal betrayal."

"How long has it been since you've seen him?" Alicia asked as she watched Orlando blow on the hot tea before taking a sip.

"Ten years," he said in a voice so low she could hardly hear him. "Sometimes I wonder which of us suffered more—him or me. Alfredo had invested a lot of time and effort in my career. Not to mention cold, hard cash. See, along with my trainer, Alfredo had half my contract, just so no funny business would happen. We split it fifty-fifty. Things were really looking good until—" He stopped, set down the teacup, and for a long moment seemed to be in another world, a world of pain and guilt.

"Until what?" Alicia finally asked, squeezing his hand gently.

"I don't . . . like to talk about it," Orlando said hesitantly.

Now it was Alicia's turn to sit silently as the clock in the corner ticked loudly. "Orlando," she said at last, "I hardly know you. But I do know this. It's a good thing to talk about whatever weighs most heavily on your heart." She leaned forward. "I know your faith in God is strong. You probably depend on Him for everything. But isn't it possible that God might bring someone into your life to help you? Maybe I'm that person," she continued as Orlando looked at her, his eyes glistening with tears. "Maybe God sent me to help you heal some of that pain."

Maybe He did, Orlando thought. *Maybe this woman is an angel in disguise.* He swallowed hard. "The night I won the title, I . . . I almost killed a man," he said, stumbling over his words and the emotions that were attached to that moment in the ring, a moment etched in his mind, began to replay with vivid clarity. "He's still in a coma. I don't think I ever prayed so hard in my life, but he never came out. So I walked away from the ring forever. Alfredo and I finally got a shot at some real money, and I gave it all up. I had been planning to move into the heavyweight ranks, like Holyfield did after he won the one-hundred-and-ninety-pound title. I really didn't have the size to compete with the big boys, but I was caught up in it all."

He turned to Alicia, their hands still joined across the table. "I don't know," he said softly. "Seeing that guy lying on the mat changed me . . . it changed me forever. Sometimes I wonder what might have happened if I'd kept on fighting, a one-hundred-and-ninety-pound cruiser up against those two-hundred-and-thirty-pound human howitzers. Maybe I would have ended up on that mat or in a hospital with tubes coming out of me. Maybe God was trying to tell me something. Maybe He was trying to save my life. I don't know. I guess I just would have muscled up and gone for it. But I decided to fight another war instead, a war for souls."

"And your brother?" Alicia asked. "He didn't understand?"

Orlando shook his head. "I never saw him again," he revealed. "I didn't even know where to look. My mother says that she knows where he is, but that it's better that she keeps it from me." He pulled his hand away to dry his eyes, taking a gulp of tea and trying to pull himself together. This afternoon wasn't exactly going as he had expected. He wanted to make an impression, and here he was, crying like a baby.

"Maybe she's right," he added after a moment, "but I'll tell you one thing. I miss Alfredo." He reached over to pick up a black-and-white photo of his father as a young man, wearing a double-breasted suit and a fedora cocked at a rakish angle. "I miss him almost as much as I miss my dad."

Alicia leaned over, and for the next few minutes, they stared in silence at the picture in his hand, each thinking about what was and what could have been.

CHAPTER EIGHT

ORLANDO SAT IN HIS OFFICE, FILLING OUT WHAT SEEMED like an endless stream of paperwork for the funding and tax-exempt status of the youth center while outside the door, the happy chaos of rambunctious children continued unabated. His mind, still a little foggy from last night's late shift at the hotel, had just started to wander back to his afternoon meeting with Alicia two days before when he heard a soft knock from the hallway.

"Come in," he said, expecting another child with a scuffed knee or a teenager with one of the seemingly endless laments about friends or family. He counted it a blessing that everyone at the youth center seemed to trust him with secrets, although there were times he wished there weren't quite so many burdens to share.

"Hope I'm not interrupting anything," said a familiar voice from the doorway.

Orlando's head shot up at the sound, a broad grin spreading across his face. Alicia stood framed in the light from the outside corridor, a cardboard box in her arms.

"Not at all, not at all," Orlando insisted, rising quickly from his chair. "I was just thinking . . ." He stopped and then stammered, "That is, I was . . . hoping I might hear from you again . . . when you had something to show me, that is."

"Well, that's why I'm here," she said, crossing the room and setting the box down on his desk. "I needed a second opinion from someone with firsthand knowledge." From the box she carefully removed a large object wrapped in a cloth and set it upright on the desk. With a small "Ta-da!" she unveiled a rough but remarkably accurate bust of Orlando's father.

For a long moment he stared. *I better not start crying again,* he thought sternly. *She's going to think I'm some kind of wimp.* Swallowing hard, he looked from the sculpture to its creator. "It's magnificent," he managed to get out. "I can't believe you captured him so perfectly just from photographs."

"Well, not exactly," admitted Alicia.

"What do you mean?" asked Orlando.

"Well," she replied, pointing to the bust, "look closely. Like I said before, without the mustache and the eyeglasses, and if you make the nose just a little bit smaller, it's a spitting image of you." She smiled. "You guys are regular bookends."

"I guess you're right," Orlando acknowledged, even as a fresh idea was forming in his mind. "Alicia," he continued, "there's something I'd like to ask you. A way you might be able to help the cause around here."

"Name it," Alicia responded promptly.

The next evening, Alicia, dressed in her best outfit, with her long, lustrous hair in a bun, sat opposite a group of dour businessmen, wondering if it had been such a good idea to volunteer without actually knowing what she was getting herself into. The conference room of the youth center was, in stark contrast to the rest of the building, a quiet and somber place far removed from the ruckus at the other end of the main hall and a place where business was the order of the day.

In the center of the large conference table, the bust of Orlando

Leone Sr. was displayed on a small pedestal. Across from the group of stern-faced men in gray suits, Orlando had assembled a team that included her, his mother, and his lawyer, Pete. Looking at the expressions on the men across from them, Alicia couldn't help feeling that Orlando and his small squad were already outnumbered by this solemn battalion of bankers, attorneys, and investors.

On an easel behind where they sat, Orlando had propped up a large architectural rendering of a multistoried building in an urban setting. With a speaking style that combined his best pulpit delivery with a straightforward sales pitch, Orlando was appealing directly to the hearts of his audience—a tactic Alicia wasn't at all sure would work since she seriously doubted these men possessed the organs in question.

"Although much volunteer work has already been graciously donated by many dedicated people," Orlando was saying, "I'm sure you gentlemen realize that we still need a substantial infusion of funds to begin our preliminary renovation of the existing facility."

An older man with a florid face and a fringe of hair around his shiny bald head cleared his throat. "What about the million dollars raised so far?" he demanded. "What happened to all that?"

"I'm glad you asked that," Orlando responded smoothly as he turned to a pair of deeply tanned men, obviously a father and son, who were sitting by themselves at the far end of the large oval table. "Mr. McCracken and his sons, who are contractors, have been very cooperative with us in putting together initial budgets and feasibility studies on a prorated basis. But as I'm sure you all know, it takes a good deal of start-up capital to get a project of this size under way."

"And we've still got the youth center to run," Geneva interjected as she stood up next to her son. "It costs between forty and forty-two thousand dollars a month to keep this facility operational, gentlemen," she explained. Alicia couldn't help being impressed by the older woman's smooth delivery. Now she knew where Orlando got his chops.

"And that's just the amount we need to keep the doors open," she continued. Then, leaning forward with her hands resting on the table, she looked each and every businessman, one after the other, in the eyes and said, "This is a serious job we're trying to accomplish here, gentlemen. We're trying to keep kids off the street, kids who might otherwise be pointing a gun in your face and sticking their hands in your pockets." She pounded her fist on the table for emphasis. "We believe that the gospel can change lives and turn a troubled kid into a productive member of society. But we've got to have the means to reach them with God's Word on a continuous, day-by-day basis. And that's where you all come in."

Another potential investor raised his hand. "How much are we ultimately talking about here?" he asked.

"The figure is a nice round one," said Orlando, stepping forward with a smile. "Twenty million dollars." He held up his hand, counting off his points, finger by finger. "That will provide day care for working mothers; classrooms for adult education and kids who have dropped out; recreational facilities to help kids develop their bodies and their sense of team spirit and fair play."

Orlando's voice took on a new intensity as the passion he felt for his mission began to surge. "I know what you're thinking," he continued. "You're wondering, if the Bible says the gospel is free, why am I up here asking you for money? Well, let me put it this way. The Word of God may be free, but the preaching of God's Word isn't. It takes money to spread the good news. Ask any pastor who's tried to put together a building fund for a new church.

Ask any administrator who's trying to keep a drug rehab program or a home for unwed mothers functioning. It all takes cash, lots of cash, and that's where you come in. You're the people God has blessed with wealth and the ability to create wealth. This is your community, the city where you live and where you raise your children. If you won't help, who will?"

As Orlando fixed them all with an intense stare, some of the assembled men began squirming in their seats, while others nodded and smiled in agreement with his words. Orlando pointed to the bust of his father and spoke again in a clear and concise tone of voice that drew and held the attention of everyone in the room.

"This sculpture of my father," he told them, "is going to be a symbol of what we're trying to accomplish in this city. Some of you knew Orlando Leone Sr., some of you worked with him, and many of you contributed to his early efforts to provide a place of refuge for the youth of our community." He turned to Alicia. "Here is the talented young artist Alicia Corbin, who gave of her time and ability to create this symbol, a point of identification we can all rally around. Her life, too, was affected by the work at the center."

Alicia nodded and stood briefly to acknowledge the applause of the gathering. She cast a grateful glance in Orlando's direction. She knew exactly what he was doing by calling attention to her and her work. These men could afford to pay top dollar for what they wanted, and if they decided they wanted something made by her, there was no better recommendation than word of mouth.

With a few words of encouragement and appeal, Orlando brought the meeting to an end, and Alicia was gratified to find more than one of the seemingly stuffy businessmen coming up to her afterward to offer his congratulations on her work. Geneva and Pete followed the others out, still talking up the project and leaving Orlando and Alicia alone in the suddenly empty room. For a moment both were at a loss for words, yet the smile they shared spoke louder of what they felt for each other than anything they might have said. Finally Orlando broke the spell by looking at his watch.

"Oh, boy," he said with disappointment. "I've got to be at work in a couple of hours." He stuck out his hand. "Alicia," he said, "thanks for everything. Your being here tonight meant a lot to me."

"No," replied Alicia, taking his hand and shaking it warmly, "thank you. Thank you for all you've done for Darla." She blushed as the words came to her lips involuntarily. "And for me." She stepped back and picked up her purse from the chair beside her. "Please," she said, "don't let me stop you."

When she turned, she found Orlando fixing her with a stare that sent a warm tingle up her spine. *He wants to ask me something,* she thought, *but he can't find the words.*

"Yes?" she said helpfully. "Is there something you want to say, Orlando?"

He smiled, secretly pleased that she had read his thoughts. "There's something I want to show you," he told her. "Someplace I should have taken you to before now." He stepped forward, slipping on his suit jacket. "Will you take a little ride with me?" he asked.

"I thought you had to go to work," she replied.

"It's right down the street," he answered. "We can be there in five minutes." He picked up her coat and held it out for her.

"Let's go," she said, smiling as she slipped her arms into the sleeves. "I can't wait."

Three blocks and five minutes later, Alicia found herself wondering what she was supposed to get so excited about. Orlando had taken her down a particularly ramshackle street, lined with one boarded-up and broken-down building after the other, stopping finally at a large parking lot behind a locked chain-link fence. Taking a key ring from his pocket, he opened the gate and stepped inside, turning and bowing as if he were inviting her into a royal reception hall. In the distance, Alicia could make out the looming shape of a huge abandoned hospital building, its windows blocked with plywood and its main entrance filled with old newspapers and other street debris. She studied the proud look on Orlando's face, then turned back to the building, a place obviously deserted for several years.

"It's . . . very nice," she said dubiously.

Orlando laughed, the sound echoing through the empty lot. A sudden wind caught the shreds of newspapers and blew them up into the night sky. Alicia could not remember ever being in a more desolate and unwelcoming place. "What do you see?" Orlando asked her.

"Well," Alicia replied, deciding that honesty was probably the best policy. "To tell you the truth, I see an old broken-down hospital that probably should have been demolished years ago."

"Of course you do," Orlando responded with a wide grin. "Now ask me what I see."

"Okay," said Alicia, going along with his playful mood. "What do you see?"

"I see the Orlando Leone Sr. Youth Center," he announced loudly and, turning back to face the building, threw his arms out wide. "I see a dream come true."

Now it was Alicia's turn to laugh. "Maybe you better keep dreaming for a while, Orlando," she said skeptically.

He turned back to her, a brilliant light burning in his eyes, and grabbed her by both shoulders. "Don't you see, Alicia?" he asked intently. "This is it! This is where we make it happen. Sure, you can look at it and just see the shell of the old All Saints Hospital. You can see an eyesore waiting to be destroyed. But what I see is a place where kids and adults can come to be healed and helped. I see a place where a community can finally come together and meet God face-to-face." He laughed again. "I also see a place that's got my name written on the bill of sale."

"You don't mean—" Alicia began.

Orlando nodded vigorously. "That's exactly what I mean," he interjected. "It's taken every last penny that I made as a fighter—three million dollars—but I bought this particular white elephant right out from under the noses of seven land developers who wanted to turn it into some kind of high-priced shopping complex. Can you imagine that?" he asked, still holding tightly to her shoulders. "Who is going to be able to afford shopping around here?"

"Whoa!" Alicia exclaimed, taking a step back and holding up her hands. "Let me get this straight. You bought an abandoned hospital for three million dollars? You gave up money you could have had for retirement? For the security of you and your mother? For your future?"

"Yes!" he cried exultantly. "Isn't it wonderful?"

"I can think of another word for it," she said, folding her arms across her chest.

"No, Alicia," Orlando insisted. "I know what you're thinking, but I'm not crazy. This is the dream my father had." He pointed to the graffiti-covered entrance. "That's why I want your sculpture to be the first thing people see when they come in. That's why I'm trying to raise twenty million dollars. That's what it's going to cost to get this place up and running. That's why I'm working a second job, to pay my living expenses so I don't have to take anything out of the ministry. Everything I have, everything I am, has gone into this place." He turned back to look at the dilapidated building. "It may look like nothing to you," he said, then faced her again, "but to me, it's everything. It's my life's work, my purpose here on earth."

She stared at him for a long moment, trying to decide whether this strange man had lost his mind or was really serious about pursuing this impossible goal. The look in his eyes gave her the answer loudly and clearly. "Wow," she said with an added whistle. "I knew you were serious about helping people, but I didn't know you were this serious." She gestured to the rambling hulk of the hospital. "This isn't just a part of your life. It *is* your life."

Orlando nodded emphatically. "Now you're getting it," he said. "This is what I've been put on this earth to accomplish. It's my mission, my calling. It's what my dad was working his whole life to accomplish, and it's what I need to finish while there's still time. I mean," he said with a chuckle, "it'll take me my whole life."

Alicia couldn't help smiling at the utter intensity and seriousness radiating from Orlando. "You are one unique individual, Orlando Leone Jr.," she said. "I don't think I've ever met anyone quite like you. No wonder Darla loves you so much. You must be one of the only adults she knows who walks it like he talks it."

Orlando's smile matched the radiance of Alicia's. "Kids always know if you're for real or not," he agreed. "I have to live out what I believe, every day of my life, right in front of their eyes. If God's provision isn't real to me, it's not going to be real for them either."

"Well, no one could ever accuse you of not being real," Alicia said.

"You can't preach what you don't know," Orlando explained. "And you can't lead where you won't go." He held out his hand, and when she took it, he walked with her out of the parking lot, locking the gate behind him.

For a moment they strolled in silence until Alicia finally spoke up. "So," she said, "you made all that money fighting? Three million dollars is a fortune where I come from."

"That was nothing," replied Orlando. "It's just what I had left over after everyone got his cut, including Uncle Sam. The gross was phenomenal."

"You must have been good," Alicia observed. She knew nothing about boxing, but couldn't help being impressed with Orlando's earning power.

"I was all right," he replied modestly. "Better than some, not as good as others."

"Did you ever have a . . ." Alicia hesitated, trying to remember. "A TOK?"

Orlando laughed. "You mean a TKO? Sure, a few times. Why do you ask?"

"Because," she replied, "you just don't look like the kind of person who would go around knocking people out."

"Oh, really," said Orlando, raising his eyebrows. "And how should I look?"

"I don't really know," admitted Alicia. "Maybe you should have bigger muscles or something."

"Excuse me," answered Orlando in mock offense. "But my muscles are plenty big enough, young lady. Besides, all the punching power you need to knock someone out doesn't come from big muscles."

"Where does it come from?" she wanted to know.

"In the movement of your hips," he explained, "not your

arms. It's the way you rotate your hips that puts the power into your punch."

"Are you sure?" Alicia asked doubtfully.

"I ought to know," Orlando replied. "I used to do it for a living."

"So," continued Alicia, gently teasing, "do you think I could knock someone out?"

Orlando replied playfully, "With those hips, you could definitely knock out fools on a world-class level."

Alicia, flirting along, said, "Oh, really? Show me how to do it."

"Okay," Orlando said as he put his hands on her hips to position her. "If I may . . ."

"You may," said Alicia.

He smiled, then placed her in a boxing stance. After giving her a few pointers, he watched as she tried a little shadowboxing. As they touched and moved during the impromptu lesson, a final, thin wall came down between them.

"Girl," he said, impressed, "I wouldn't want to meet you in a dark alley."

"Really?" squealed the delighted Alicia, still punching the air.

"I wouldn't lie to you," he replied. "Well, actually, you might be the only dark-alley encounter I'd look forward to." Alicia stopped punching and smiled at Orlando. After a brief pause, he said, "Hold on just a second" and headed toward his car.

"What are you doing?" she asked.

Orlando made no reply. Instead, he opened all the car doors, turned the key in the ignition, turned on the headlights, and cranked up the stereo. Shortly, the Santana hit "Smooth" began to boom through the car's CD player. Orlando returned to his new sparring partner, who was puzzled by his actions. Reading this on her face, Orlando explained, "I figured anybody with as many natural moves as you have must know how to salsa."

With a laugh, Alicia responded, "You know I do prego, boy." They began to dance in the glow from the headlights, laughing and joking like two teenagers skipping school. "Do all preachers dance like this?" she inquired.

"Only the really good ones," he assured her, and they began to laugh again. Suddenly, they stopped dancing and shared their first kiss. For a moment, they were two people with no responsibilities in the world. Only love and passion. By the time the song ended, Orlando's heart was completely gone, and so was Alicia's.

CHAPTER NINE

AFTER GETTING ALICIA SAFELY BACK TO HER CAR AT THE youth center and on her way home, Orlando made several short-cuts through the city he knew so well, arriving at the front entrance of the hotel in a slight daze with minutes to spare for the beginning of his late shift.

Even from a half block away, he could immediately see that tonight was going to be anything but routine for the security crew. News vans mounted with satellite dishes jammed the front driveway, and bright lights glared over the heads of a large crowd gathered in the lobby. Pushing through the bodies, Orlando made his way to the front desk, shouting to the clerk to be heard over the uproar.

"Let me guess," he said. "The champ has arrived."

"You got that right," the clerk answered. "He just checked in. Took the whole top floor."

Orlando nodded, less impressed with the arrival of the heavy-weight champion of the world than he was concerned about making sure his security staff was in place and on alert.

As if to underscore that concern, the hotel manager pushed his way through the crush of reporters and took Orlando to one side of the reception desk. As Orlando watched, Dexter pushed himself to the front as well, using his substantial girth to clear a path before him.

"We've got to get all these people out of here, Orlando," the manager demanded. "This is a fire hazard, and the last thing we need is a bunch of official types swarming over the place." He wiped the sweat from his face with a large white handkerchief. "I hate it when these big shots just show up unannounced," he fretted. "I mean, champion or not, the guy acts like he owns the place."

"So tell him to look for another hotel," suggested Orlando.

The manager gave him an incredulous look. "Are you kidding?" he said. "You can't buy this kind of publicity."

At that moment Dexter arrived, looking out of breath and more than a little spooked by the mob of reporters.

"Relax, everybody," Orlando said reassuringly. "Everything's under control." He turned to Dexter. "Did you call in Scott and Dean for duty tonight like I asked?" Dexter nodded. He looked around. "And is Chris in position?"

Dexter nodded again. "He's watching the elevators," he explained.

"Good," Orlando replied, nodding with satisfaction. "Now you wait here for me. I'll be back in five."

Returning as promised and dressed in his security blazer, Orlando, with the help of Dexter, quickly got the hotel lobby under control, cordoning off the reporters to one side of the large room and allowing legitimate guests to check in at the front desk.

"Can I have your attention, ladies and gentlemen?" he said in a loud, clear voice of authority. Immediately the press contingent, expecting news, quieted down. "I have it on good authority," he explained, "that Mr. Vasquez will not be leaving his room tonight." A groan went up from the assembled reporters, and Orlando held up his hands for silence. "I can assure you," he continued, "that any of you who are planning to camp out in the lobby here will be in for a very uneventful evening. I have to ask you now to vacate the premises unless you plan on being our guests here this evening. Otherwise, if you feel you must stay as part of your job, then we've made an accommodation outside the lobby doors where you can gather as long as your presence doesn't disturb our registered guests. Is that clear?"

Muttering and mumbling greeted the question as the reporters and news crews began moving as a herd toward the front entrance. One reporter stood away from the rest, speaking rapidly into the camera as she tried to dash off a late-breaking report of the champ's whereabouts before being escorted out of the hotel.

That image was playing across town on Alicia's television when the phone rang. Setting down her sketching charcoal, she answered it, resting the receiver on her shoulder and continuing to work as she listened with increasing impatience to the voice on the other end of the line.

"Listen, Kathleen," she said, finally breaking in, "he's very likable, okay? That's all there is to know. You're not changing my mind on this."

"Get a grip, girl," snapped Kathleen, lying on her bed propped up on pillows and applying cold cream to her face. "I mean, this dude is living on a whole other planet from you and me. Just listen to yourself."

"No," replied the exasperated Alicia. "You know what, Kathleen? I'm tired of listening to myself, and I'm tired of listening to you. That's all I've been hearing for as long as I can remember, and I'm beginning to think, between the two of us, we don't have enough sense to come in out of the rain."

"Speak for yourself," sniffed Kathleen, then added in an ominous tone, "I'll tell you now, Alicia. If you go and get yourself too carried away with this youth center thing and this man's world, I can guarantee that things are going to change between us."

"What is that," demanded an irate Alicia, "a threat? You know me too well for that. I don't respond to petty blackmail, Kathleen. Especially coming from my friend."

A long silence followed from the other end of the line. "You're changing, Alicia," Kathleen said at last. "You know that?"

"Maybe I am," replied Alicia. "And that's probably the most encouraging thing you've said to me all week." She was trying her best to convey the feelings that had come over her in the past several days—feelings of excitement and expectation as if she were a small child awaiting Christmas morning. But it just wasn't working.

"You best be careful, girl," Kathleen said in a voice that had suddenly grown cold and hard. "Or else you're going to find yourself out there all alone, with no way to get back and no one to get back to."

"Kathleen, don't talk like that. I'll be all right. I know you love me, but I'll take my chances." Alicia's reply was terse as she hung up. Only then did she notice how she had spoiled the sketch she had been working on with several dark scrawling lines. She sighed, feeling just as alone as Kathleen had predicted. Quickly, before she could talk herself out of it, she picked up the phone and dialed a number.

"Orlando Leone," she said when she was connected to the front desk.

"One moment, please," the operator responded, but the line emitted the forlorn sound of a busy signal. "Shall I leave a message?" asked the operator.

"No," replied Alicia. "Don't bother."

At the desk in the security office, Dexter held the receiver in his hand. "It's the guests in room twenty-six twenty-one," he reported to Orlando. "They're complaining about the noise coming from the penthouse. That's the fifth complaint the last half hour," he added as he hung up the phone. "They want us to give them back their money and find them another hotel."

"All right, Dex," an unruffled Orlando replied. "It's time to earn all those free meals you've been cadging from the kitchen. Head on up to the champ's room and respectfully ask them to keep the noise down."

Dexter almost choked on the ice-cream bar he was eating. "Me?" he asked incredulously. But the look on his boss's face told him there was no use in arguing.

Orlando watched as Dexter trudged to the door and out into the hall, then returned to what he was doing before the interruption. Straightening his tie, he put on a sunny smile and said out loud, "Alicia! What do you say you and I go out and grab—" He scowled. "No," he muttered to himself before he tried another approach. "Miss Corbin," he said with stiff formality, "I wonder if I might have the pleasure of—no!" He sighed and rested his chin on his hand. It had been a long time since he'd actually asked a woman for anything. And now here he was, trying to figure out a way to tell her he wanted to be a part of her life.

Dexter was reluctantly crossing the lobby, considering for a moment a brief stop at the buffet table before deciding that Orlando wouldn't exactly approve. Shuffling to the elevator, he pushed the button and waited for the door to slide open. As it was about to close, five garishly costumed musicians in full mariachi regalia pushed their way in and crowded Dexter to the back of the elevator. Speaking rapidly to one another, they hardly noticed the miserable-looking security guard who took the ride up to the penthouse floor with them.

The elevator let Dexter and his fellow passengers out onto a scene of wild abandon. A scorching Latin beat boomed down the hall from a stereo turned up full blast, and every door on the top floor seemed to be opened wide. As he passed down the hall, the mariachi band following close behind, Dexter caught a glimpse of one wild party scene after another through each doorway. Beautiful women with vacant eyes rubbed elbows with cigar-chomping sports promoters and high rollers with slicked-back hair and shiny silk suits. Pungent smoke hung heavy in the air, and bottles of expensive liquor sat half empty on the hallway carpet. Room service trays with half-eaten steaks and whole lobsters were stacked on top of each other on every available surface. Around one corner, a group of men hunkered down on the floor for an on-the-spot, high-stakes crap game.

As Dexter approached the champ's suite of spacious rooms, he could hear the sounds of a loud argument and entered just in time to see two men pushing and shoving each other. The drunker one grabbed a champagne bottle and smashed it against the wall, sending the bubbly liquid showering over the room. Two women in a tight embrace with a man on the couch screamed as they were soaked, and loud laughter came through the double doors that led to the main room of the suite.

Dexter singled out a partygoer who seemed at least semi-coherent and crossed the room to talk to him. The music was so loud that even shouting at the top of his lungs, he couldn't make himself understood until the man bellowed out, "Turn the music down!" at an even more deafening volume than the relentless beat coming from the sound system.

"Thank you, sir," Dexter said gratefully. He took a deep breath and continued, "I'm sorry to disturb your celebration but—"

The man seemed to look right past him into the other room and with an exuberant shout pointed to the mariachi band, setting up in one corner. "Olé! Olé!" he shouted as the band started pumping out a Mexican dance tune.

"Excuse me," Dexter said, raising his voice slightly, only to be completely ignored by the man, who had begun to form a conga line. "Um, excuse me." The dancers started snaking around the room, one of them bumping into the guard and staggering away. "Hey, tubby," he said in a slurred voice. "Are you going to dance or just stand in the way?" At that moment, Dexter found himself surrounded by three of the champ's beefy security guards who quietly, efficiently, and forcefully moved him out of the suite and back into the hallway.

Downstairs in the security room, Orlando was pacing up and down trying to work up the nerve for his next move. Finally, taking a deep breath and throwing up a quick prayer, he grabbed the telephone and punched in a string of numbers. As the phone rang, Orlando felt his whole world slowing to a complete stop. He waited in suspended animation, not knowing whether to work through his nervousness or just hang up and admit he was too much of a coward to try to make a connection with such a beautiful woman.

"Hello," he heard Alicia's voice on the other end say, and suddenly his heart was in his mouth.

"Hello, Alicia," he stammered. "It's me . . . Orlando."

A moment of silence followed. "Orlando," Alicia said at last. "I was just thinking about you. That is . . . I was wondering how you were doing."

"I'm doing fine," he answered before lamely adding, "and how about you?"

"Fine," she answered in a halting tone. "Just fine."

An embarrassed pause ensued during which he racked his brains for something clever to say. With nothing coming to mind, he took another deep breath and plunged ahead.

"Alicia," he said, "I was wondering—"

"Yes?" she replied, but he was too nervous to hear the eagerness in her voice.

At that moment, at the worst of all possible times, Dexter burst through the door. His face was beaded with sweat and his uniform was crumpled. "Boss," he said breathlessly. "We've got a problem up there."

Orlando sighed. Duty was most definitely calling. "Alicia," he said into the receiver, "can I . . . that is . . . I need to call you back."

"All right," she said. Once again Orlando was too distracted to hear the disappointment in her voice.

Hanging up, Orlando turned angrily to Dexter. "I send you up there to do a simple job, and what happens?" he scolded. "You come running back here with your tail between your legs."

"You don't know what it's like up there, boss," Dexter protested. "I was lucky to get out alive!"

Orlando rose and slipped on his blazer. "Never mind," he said. "Find Scott, and meet me in the lobby in three minutes."

As soon as the elevator door opened on the penthouse floor, Orlando, along with Dexter and the veteran guard named Scott, stepped into the smoke-filled hallway. He knew then that he should have taken care of this particular piece of business by himself instead of sending the overweight and good-natured Dexter to do the job. *I need to focus on my responsibilities,* Orlando chided himself, *instead of sitting around thinking up ways to get back to Alicia.*

Striding purposefully down the corridor, Orlando and his team entered the penthouse suite. Taking a quick look around to size up the situation, he crossed to the mariachi band and pulled the trumpet out from between the player's lips exactly in the middle of a squealing solo. The other members stopped playing and milled around in confusion. In the sudden silence, Orlando turned to find that everyone in the room was standing and staring at him.

"Ladies and gentlemen," he announced in his most authoritative voice, "you are entirely too rowdy. As difficult as this may be for you to accept, there are guests on the floors directly beneath you, and on either side, who are trying to get some sleep." He glanced at his watch and continued, "It's one o'clock in the morning. Here's the drill: anyone who is not a registered guest of this establishment needs to be out of here in two minutes. This party is now officially over."

"What if we don't feel like leaving?" shouted a belligerent voice from the back of the room.

"Then you'll be free to continue your celebration at our local precinct house," Orlando replied evenly. "C'mon, let's move it."

One of the beefy guards who had hustled Dexter out earlier swaggered up to Orlando. "Hey, man," he said. "You're spoiling our fun." He leaned over, his face inches away. "You don't want to do that, do you?"

Orlando stared back at him, unblinking. "May I see your room key, sir?" he asked politely.

"I don't got to show you nothing," the guard sneered. "I work for the heavyweight champion of the world." With a sudden thrust, he tried to shove Orlando back into the Mexican musicians, who scattered, clutching their instruments. In the next fraction of a second, Orlando, acting on an innate reflex as natural as breathing, grabbed the guard's right hand and locked it under his left armpit. He used his right hand to push the guard's elbow toward the ceiling, hyper-extending his arm. The guard yelled in pain. Then, in a seamless martial arts maneuver so fast the guests could see only a blur, he flipped the guard to the floor, slamming him hard on his side. Even before the guard could shout out a protest, Orlando was standing over him, a foot at his neck in a position that completely paralyzed him.

"Hey!" came a bellowing voice from across the room. The crowd parted to let Antonio Vasquez through. "What do you think you're doing with my boy?"

Face-to-face, Orlando locked eyes with the champion. It was clear immediately that Vasquez was more than a little drunk, but it wasn't just the alcohol that set off an alarm in Orlando's brain. There was a look in the boxer's eyes, a look Orlando had seen only too often in the ring. This man was capable of anything, he realized. Violence was the way he dealt with the world, and it was never more than a heartbeat away. Antonio Vasquez lived his life like an explosion just waiting to be triggered.

"Your party's over, Champ," Orlando said as clearly and concisely as he could. "And your boy is under arrest for attempted assault."

A light of recognition seemed to slowly dawn in the boxer's glazed eyes. "Hey," he said as if trying to talk around a swollen tongue. "Aren't you Leone?"

Orlando stepped back and freed the bodyguard, who stood up, rubbing his neck. "You know this dude?" he asked Vasquez, jerking his thumb in Orlando's direction.

"Of course, I know him, you moron," Vasquez snarled. "Everybody knows Orlando Leone. Used to be a real thing." He turned to Orlando. "Right?"

"That's not the issue tonight," Orlando replied.

"Sure," countered Vasquez. "Sure it is." He turned to face the rest of the crowd, gathered in a dumbstruck circle behind him. "Hey, everybody," he shouted. "This is Orlando Leone. He was a tough guy back in his day." He laughed, a cruel and ugly sound. "Now look at him. Got himself a little jacket and a flashlight and thinks he's some kind of hotshot."

"That's enough, Vasquez," Orlando warned. He turned to Dexter. "Call 911," he ordered in a low voice.

The champion ignored him. "We used to throw down when I was just coming up," he continued in a loud voice. "Never did fight full-out. But I do remember that sneaky overhand right. It rung my bell many a day."

"Listen, Antonio," Orlando interjected, trying to reason with the boxer, "I think you've maybe had a little too much to drink. Why don't you go to bed and sleep it off?" He gestured to the bodyguard. "Tell you what," he continued. "I'll let your buddy off the hook tonight. Let's just shut this thing down and all get a good night's sleep."

"No way," said Vasquez, shaking his head like a bull getting ready to charge. "I've got a score to settle with you, Leone. You whaled on me too many times to let you off the hook now." He raised his fist in front of Orlando's face. "Well, now I've learned a thing or two, and it looks like payback time to me. Where's that right hand tonight?"

"Don't do this, Vasquez," pleaded Orlando, even as the crowd in the room began shouting insults at him and egging on the champ. "We left those wars back in the gym. This is your last warning. Back off or I'm gonna have to take you down in front of all your groupies."

With a roar like an enraged animal, Vasquez swung at Orlando, a roundhouse right that Orlando swiftly ducked. Then, acting on experience that had been bred into him from years in the ring,

Orlando made his move—a quick, three-punch combination to the body and a blistering left-right to the face. Stung and stunned, the champ reeled back as Orlando charged him. In a single smooth motion Orlando grabbed him in a headlock and flipped him to the ground with a thud heard three floors below. Pinned beneath Orlando, Vasquez groaned and went limp. Orlando quickly cuffed him while Dexter and Scott held the bodyguards back from rushing in. While all of this was happening, hundreds of camera flashes were going off. A moment later, three uniformed policemen rushed into the room, followed by a handful of reporters who had persisted in staking out the hotel. Flashes blazed again as the officers helped Orlando manhandle Vasquez, handcuffing him and lifting him to his feet. From every corner of the suite, cell phones were being busily activated. Something big had just happened, and the news was about to spread—and spread fast.

CHAPTER TEN

ALICIA HAD WAITED AS LONG AS SHE COULD STAND IT FOR the return phone call Orlando had promised. Finally throwing caution and her female pride to the wind, she picked up the telephone receiver and punched in the hotel's number.

A busy signal greeted her, and she resisted the sudden temptation to toss the phone across the room.

At that moment the commercial break during the late night movie that she had been half watching on television was interrupted by a news flash. As the stunned Alicia watched in disbelief, the screen showed Antonio Vasquez being led out of the hotel lobby's door and into the back of a waiting squad car. At the head of the phalanx of cops was Orlando Leone Jr.

Fixed on the enraged and battered face of the champ in the backseat, the cameras followed the car down the driveway and out onto the street, before returning to focus on Orlando, pressed on all sides by the horde of reporters who had rushed back to the scene.

"Mr. Leone," shouted one newscaster, shoving a microphone in his face, "is it true that you were involved in a physical altercation with the heavyweight champion of the world tonight?"

"Is it true that you took him down with one punch?" shouted

another, who was echoed by a chorus of voices asking the same question.

"You used to be a boxer," said a woman with a television station logo on the pocket of her suit jacket. "Was there some kind of a grudge between you two?"

Alicia watched spellbound and, noticing the bewildered and overwhelmed look on Orlando's face, wondered whether she should drop everything and rush down to the hotel. *He probably needs a friend,* she thought, even as the hotel manager pushed his way to the front of the crowd and spoke directly into the cameras.

"Orlando Leone is the head of security for this hotel," he said, putting his arm around Orlando. "And he's a great asset to our establishment. But he's also a former cruiserweight boxing champion . . . ," he continued, pausing for effect before crowing, "with an undefeated record!"

The reporters erupted into pandemonium as Orlando threw a dirty look at the manager and tried his best to stay calm in the crush of shouting faces and blinding lights.

The broadcast cut from the front of the hotel to the television studio where an anchorman was being handed a piece of paper. As Alicia watched, he turned to the cameras, barely able to contain his excitement.

"For those of you just tuning in," he reported in an urgent tone, "we have this extraordinary news straight from the Centennial Suites here in our city." The camera pulled in tight as he continued, "It seems that the heavyweight champion of the world, Antonio Vasquez, has just been arrested and taken into police custody. The charges are not clear at this time, but in a related development unconfirmed reports have been coming in that there was a confrontation of some sort in the hotel's penthouse suite and that a security guard single-handedly subdued the champion with one punch and then assisted police in taking him into custody."

The anchorman stopped suddenly, listening to instructions coming in over his earpiece. "We're going to take you back to the Centennial Suites now with more on this incredible story."

The broadcast flashed back to the hotel lobby, where a reporter had buttonholed an uncomfortable-looking Orlando and was grilling him on the evening's events.

"I have here thirty-nine-year-old Orlando Leone," said the frenetic reporter, talking into the camera, "a former boxer who retired with the cruiserweight championship crown in 1991." Leaning in close to Orlando with the microphone, he continued his relentless questions: "Can you tell us exactly what happened here tonight, Mr. Leone, and how it came about that you single-handedly knocked out the heavyweight champion of the world with a single blow?"

"It wasn't like that at all," Orlando countered, clearly annoyed at the manner in which the story was taking on a life of its own. "First of all, I didn't knock him out. I just" —he searched for the right word— "disabled him for a minute until the police arrived. Second, Vasquez seemed to have had a little too much to drink and was obviously not in top form. And third, I was only doing my job, which is to keep order in this hotel and protect our guests from any undue harassment or annoyance."

The reporter turned back to the camera. "There you have it, folks," he said. "Harassed and annoyed, a simple security guard fearlessly took on the heavyweight champion of the world. This is a modern David and Goliath story if I've ever heard one."

"Wait a minute," protested Orlando. "I never said—"

"What if the champ asks for a rematch?" demanded the reporter. "Will you answer the challenge?"

Orlando couldn't help laughing at the bizarre twists the story was beginning to take. "There isn't going to be a rematch," he said, "because there was no match to begin with."

The reporter once again turned to the camera. "Laughing in the face of boxing's world championship, folks," he gushed breathlessly. "This is extraordinary bravado even for this brave man."

"Look," said Orlando, trying vainly to regain control over the interview, "I told you . . . I was just doing my job as head of security."

But the reporter seemed to be ignoring him completely. "The boxing world may well have a new head honcho," he declared. "And somewhere in this city tonight, an insecure champ is running scared." He turned to ask Orlando another question. "Is it true—" he began before realizing that his interview subject had walked away in disgust.

Even taking side streets and alleyways back to the youth center, Orlando felt that he was being shadowed by the relentless news-hounds who wanted only to distort and embellish something he would just as soon forget about. Slipping into the back door of the center, he headed straight for his office where he settled down onto the couch without even bothering to take off his tie or shoes. By the time his head hit the well-worn cushion, Orlando was sound asleep.

As exhausted as he was, Orlando's sleep was troubled that night with fevered dreams of boxing rings and blinding flashes from cameras and the champ's leering face.

Waking with a start as the sun poured in through the blinds, Orlando rose wearily to his feet and, after washing his face in the boys' room of the main hall, realized how hungry he was. It seemed as if he hadn't eaten all day, and grabbing his wallet, he headed out for the diner where he knew the counterman, Boyd, would be brewing up a fresh pot of strong coffee.

Within a block of his destination, Orlando realized that, whatever else the day was going to bring, it wouldn't be a peaceful meal at his favorite greasy spoon. The crowd of reporters milling around the door of the diner assured him of that. He was just about to duck down a side street to find another place for breakfast when one of the newshounds spotted him. Within seconds, the entire pack had descended on him.

"How did you guys know where I was going to be?" he asked, mystified.

The reporters shared a cynical laugh. "Oh, we know all about you, Mr. Leone," one of them replied. "We've had all night to get our act together."

Resigned now to the clamoring escort that trailed behind him, Orlando pushed into the diner, where even more news crews were encamped. Through the crowd, he spotted Boyd behind the counter and, sitting on a stool, his lawyer, Pete.

As Orlando pushed his way to the front of the diner, Pete stood up and shouted to be heard over the flurry of questions. "Please, everyone," he said, holding up his hands. "May I have your attention, please?" When the crowd completely ignored him, Pete put two fingers to his lips and let loose with a deafening whistle. In the surprised silence that followed, he continued, "I am Mr. Leone's legal adviser. If you have any questions for my client, please address them directly to me."

Momentarily thrown off Orlando's scent, the horde descended on Pete, allowing his client a chance to take his seat at the counter. "Well, Champ," said Boyd, arriving with a steaming pot of fragrant coffee, "looks like you've had quite a night."

"Yeah, very funny," Orlando growled as he held out his cup. "This is a nightmare."

"It may be a nightmare," observed Boyd. "But it's a nightmare starring you." He laughed. "Relax, old buddy. Your fifteen minutes of fame seem to have arrived. Might as well enjoy it while it lasts." He poured out the coffee. "Go ahead," he encouraged Orlando. "It's on the house."

From his days as a fast-rising contender in the prizefighting world, Orlando had gotten a taste of what life in the public eye could be like, but there was nothing that could have quite prepared him for the onslaught of instant celebrity that confronted him around every corner and through every door that day. Returning after a hurried breakfast to the youth center, he found the street front clogged with TV trucks and on-the-spot reporters creating a gauntlet he had to run in order to get inside the center. There, down in the basement rec room, he found most of his staff and nearly all the kids gathered around the television watching a morning news report.

"Yesterday," the reporter was saying, "he was a has-been boxer who worked as a hotel security guard. Today, Orlando Leone Jr. is a name on everyone's lips, thanks to an extraordinary chain of events that has catapulted him into headlines worldwide."

As soon as the crowd in the rec room noticed his presence, he was surrounded with people he had known and worked with just the day before now treating him like a star who had dropped in from Hollywood for a surprise visit. Anxious to get away from all the attention, he hurried back upstairs and, slipping through the back door, headed for his mother's nearby apartment.

Geneva greeted him at the door with a wide-eyed stare, and as he began to speak, she quickly put her finger over her lips to keep him quiet and pointed to the television through the doorway in the living room.

There, black-and-white photos of his days as a fighter flashed by as an anchorman narrated the story all over again. "The thirty-nine-year-old bachelor," the reporter droned on, "has now become the biggest sensation in the world of sports after knocking out sports legend Antonio Vasquez, the recently crowned heavyweight champion of the world, in an alleged fracas at the hotel where Leone worked." The reporter's face appeared on-screen. "We'll be back with much more on this remarkable story after these words," he said.

The spell of the television broken for a moment, Geneva turned around to talk to her son. "Orlando?" she called. "Orlando?" The door to the apartment was wide open, and he was long gone, trying to find someplace to hide from his own image.

But it wouldn't be easy. Walking down a busy city street, he passed an appliance store with a stacked bank of televisions in the window. A crowd of people had gathered around as the multiple screens flashed dozens of pictures of Orlando. "Leone is currently employed as the head of security for the Centennial Suites Hotel," said the voice of a radio announcer over a boom box held by a teenager on his shoulder. "It was there that a party hosted by Antonio Vasquez got quote 'out of hand' unquote."

As segments of Orlando's interview from the night before were sliced in, he could hear himself saying, "I was only doing my job, which is to keep order in this hotel and protect our guests from any undue harassment or annoyance." He hailed a cab and jumped in the backseat at the exact moment that one of the crowd turned to notice the newly minted celebrity in the flesh.

"Hey," the shout went up, "it's him!" Eyes turned toward the cab even then disappearing down the block.

Orlando hunched low in the seat, hoping to avoid the notice of the cabdriver, who had his radio tuned to an all-sports talk show. "Orlando Leone is remembered by many," the host was saying, "as the former champion of the lightly regarded cruiserweight division in professional boxing, where he fought undefeated from 1977 to 1991."

The cab passed a newsstand where headlines screamed "Champ KO'd in Hotel Brawl" while on the radio a caller had just been put on the air.

"I know this guy," said a disembodied voice, "he used to hold a piece of the cruiserweight title."

"That's right," the host replied, "but there's a whole lot more to the story." Orlando groaned inwardly. He knew only too well what was coming next. "Leone was raised in a strict fundamentalist family," the host continued, sounding as if he were reading the copy from a wire service report. "He spent his early years in church or on the street evangelizing with his parents."

"But what happened to him?" asked the caller.

"Good question," the host replied. "Speculation had it that he rebelled against his heavy-handed religious upbringing, taking out his aggression in the ring."

"Drop me at the next corner," Orlando called out to the driver. He had to get away from the story of his own life, but there didn't seem to be anywhere to hide.

"Sure thing," said the driver, steering toward the curb. Then looking into the rearview mirror, he began to chatter at his passenger. "I remember that guy," he was saying. "He was the one who put that boxer Nigel Hanson in a coma, back in 1991. That was the last I ever heard of him."

"This will be fine," barked Orlando, throwing a handful of bills into the front seat and jumping out the door.

"Hey," he heard the driver call after him, "aren't you . . . ?"

Running down the street, Orlando seriously wondered whether he was about to lose his mind. *If I had it to do all over again,* he reflected bitterly, *I would never have interfered with that big lunkhead's stupid party to begin with*. But even as the thought came to his mind, he realized that, if he had it to do all over again, nothing would have changed. It was his duty, his responsibility, and those were two things he took very seriously.

Moving quickly toward an intersection, half expecting to be recognized at any moment, he was startled when a car pulled up directly in front of him and the passenger-side door flew open. "Get in!" said Pete from behind the wheel, and as Orlando made a leap into the car, he noticed for the first time a figure in the backseat. He turned to face the smiling, sympathetic eyes of Alicia.

CHAPTERELEVEN

THREE MEN SAT IN THE WHITE-CARPETED EXPANSE OF AN enormous room, sparsely furnished and decorated with large abstract canvases. A wall-sized picture window looked out over a pristine country setting where several high-end automobiles, including a Rolls-Royce and a gunmetal gray Jaguar, were parked in a sweeping circular driveway.

But the men in the room seemed to be paying no attention to the art on the walls or the view of the country estate. Their attention was fixed instead on a big-screen television in one corner of the room. As a servant bearing a silver tray softly approached to set down tall drinks on the glass-topped coffee table, expressions of anger, frustration, and pure hatred mirrored what each man was feeling about what he saw on the screen.

There, a smiling picture of Orlando Leone had appeared, standing on the steps of the youth center with several kids, including Darla, gathered around him. "These days," the announcer was saying, "Leone spends most of his time overseeing operations at the inner-city outreach center he founded, dedicated to meeting the needs of troubled and disadvantaged kids in the poor neighborhoods of the area."

The picture dissolved, replaced next by a series of video clips showing Orlando receiving a variety of community service awards and preaching from the stage of the youth center. "While most of the businesses and residents in the area applaud his efforts," the announcer continued, "there are a few who have expressed alarm at the rough and undisciplined element that is attracted to the programs offered by Leone's center."

An interview snippet with an irate man in a toupee appeared next. "Kids are always hanging around there," he complained, "and to tell you the truth, I'm not sure their parents even know what goes on behind those closed doors. We hear lots of singing and shouting. I think someone should investigate."

His dour face was replaced by a small child on the street directly in front of the center. A microphone hovered near his slightly bewildered face. "Do you ever see anything strange happening in there?" the voice of a reporter was heard to ask. "Anything that might make you feel at all uncomfortable?"

"Um . . . ," the child stammered, casting a frightened look into the camera.

"It's all right, Timmy," the reporter's voice urged the boy. "You can say yes if you want to. There's nothing to be afraid of."

"Yes," the boy echoed.

A quick cut to a newsroom showed a stern-looking anchor behind a desk. He cleared his throat and began reading from a sheaf of paper in his hands. "When asked in a newspaper profile six months ago why he was so involved in community service, Leone was quoted as saying, 'Because Jesus is coming soon.'"

Freddie was sitting on the couch. Upon hearing that last comment, his mouth hung open, and his face grew very pale. He grabbed a drink off the table and drained it in several large swallows.

"What's the matter with you?" asked Sam Freeman, noticing the haunted look on his employee's face.

"This doesn't look good for the champ. Not at all," stammered Freddie.

"Get a grip, would you?" his boss shot back, grabbing one of the drinks for himself. "I don't like nervous people around me."

"Sure thing, Mr. Freeman," Freddie replied, licking his lips and looking as if his collar was suddenly too tight around his neck.

"He's the one who should be nervous," snarled Antonio Vasquez, nursing a swollen lower lip from the uppercut he'd taken the night before. He gestured to a photo of Orlando on the screen. "I'm going to put this guy in his grave. You mark my words."

"Quiet," ordered Sam Freeman, cocking his ear toward the television. "I need to hear this. We've got to figure out where this Leone character's head is at."

On the screen, the news anchor had turned to the station's sports commentator for an inside look at the fallout in the boxing world from the news of the champ's humiliating punishment at the hands of a virtual unknown nearly twice his age.

"Any predictions for a possible rematch?" he asked, his tongue firmly planted in his cheek.

"Sure," responded the sports reporter. "Anytime Leone feels the least bit suicidal, I'm sure Vasquez would be only too happy to oblige him." He shared a laugh with the anchor before continuing, "But seriously, Bob, back when Leone was a contender, word had it that he was considering making a move out of the cruiserweight division and into the heavyweight ranks. Of course, that was before the near tragedy with Nigel Hanson took Leone out of the ring once and for all. But to tell you the truth, after ten years out of the spotlight, I very much doubt this particular comeback kid has got what it takes or wants what it takes."

"Is there any truth to the rumor," the anchor queried, "that Leone used the Hanson coma as an excuse to avoid having to fight as a heavyweight?"

The sports reporter shook his head. "I doubt it, Bob. Orlando Leone is a real rags-to-riches American saga. I think it's more likely that this attack on the champ was staged to gain publicity for his work at the youth center. Unless I'm very much mistaken, he's going to be milking this notoriety for all it's worth."

Finally unable to stand what he was viewing for another moment, Antonio Vasquez reached across the table and, grabbing the remote, shut off the television. "How come I never got that kind of press before?" he demanded of his manager.

Freeman simply shrugged. "You heard him," he said. "It's a rags-to-riches story. People love the underdog."

"Yeah, well, I'm about to run over this particular underdog," snarled Vasquez. "I defend my title six times and barely get a mention in the papers. This clown comes out of the woodwork and takes advantage of me when I'm drunk. Now he's getting all the glory, and I'm stuck looking like a total fool."

Freeman took a long, slow sip of his drink, then turned and smiled at his client. "It's a fluke, Champ," he reassured him. "That's the only reason you're seeing all this hoopla. A thousand planes take off and land every day with no problem. You never hear about them. It's the one that crashes that gets all the attention. Give it a few more days. The whole thing will blow over."

Vasquez shook his head vehemently. "No," he insisted. "They're going to remember this one." He slammed a fist into his open palm. "And they're going to remember when I lay this preacher man in his grave. No one humiliates Antonio Vasquez and lives to tell about it. *No one.*"

"Whoa, Champ," cautioned Freddie. "Take it easy."

"I'm not taking anything easy!" Vasquez shouted in a voice that rattled the plate glass of the picture window. "This guy's gonna pay and pay big. What he put me through, well . . . it's unpresidential!"

"Don't you mean unprecedented?" Freddie suggested softly.

"Yeah," replied Vasquez. "That too."

Freeman suddenly held up his hands, commanding silence. His eyes were bright with excitement, and he stood up and began to pace the room. "Look, Champ," he said in a voice that could barely hide his glee. "When it comes to business, I run the show. Not you. But when I hear a great idea, it doesn't matter where it comes from. Even if it comes from you." He leaned over and slapped the boxer on his massive shoulders. "And I think you might have just come up with a multimillion-dollar plane wreck, if you know what I mean."

"You're going to kill Leone in a plane wreck?" the champ asked hopefully.

Freeman ignored the question. "I'll bet you I can pull this off," he said more to himself than to the others in the room. "If anyone can, it's Sam Freeman."

In his small office many miles from Freeman's gleaming country mansion, Orlando sat at his desk, listening to Pete as he talked excitedly while across the room, Alicia prepared three cups of instant coffee on a small hot plate.

"Look," Pete was saying, waving his arms and prowling around the room, "I know this is very stressful right now, Orlando. Being the center of attention always is." He gestured to the building around them. "But just imagine what all this is going to do for your work here."

Orlando shook his head. "Where was all this exposure fifteen years ago when I needed it?" he asked Pete rhetorically. "It makes my skin crawl. This is not what I want to be known for. Listen," he continued intently, "I don't want to be famous. The Lord needs this kind of attention. Not me. This is the last thing I ever dreamed I'd have to deal with. I've got a job to do, and this is just getting in the way."

Pete waved away his objections. "Stuff like this doesn't come along every day," he insisted. "You've got to take advantage of the opportunities when you can. Make this work in your favor, Orlando. In God's favor, if that's the way you want to look at it. Just remember, no press is bad press."

"Oh, yeah?" countered Orlando, holding up a tabloid newspaper with a headline that read "Jesus in His Corner, Says Leone." "This is an insult!" he exclaimed. "And I'm not going to stand for it."

Alicia approached with the cups of coffee and set them down on the desk. She was about to return for the cream and sugar when Orlando grabbed her by the hand. "Alicia," he said, "I just want to say again how sorry I am that I didn't call you back last night. Things kind of got . . . out of control."

She smiled at him. "Please, Orlando," she replied. "Don't worry about it. I know you had your hands full . . . literally!" After they laughed together at Alicia's quick wit, she added reassuringly, "I'm sure everything is going to work out fine."

"You really think so?" he asked hopefully before realizing that Pete had been silently listening to every word of their conversation. "Hey," he said testily to his friend. "Haven't you got some phone calls to make or something?" he added, dropping a heavy hint.

"Oh, yeah, that's right," Pete stammered, quickly gathering up his papers and slurping his coffee as he headed for the door. "I'll be down the hall," he said as Orlando nodded impatiently. "I've got to sort out this schedule with Letterman and Oprah."

He exited, leaving Orlando and Alicia alone. A moment of silence passed before she asked tentatively, "Is he kidding?"

"I wish he was," replied Orlando, rolling his eyes. "He says they both want me to go on and tell my side of the story." He sighed. "I don't want this in my life, and it seems that no one is really listening to me."

"I am," Alicia said softly.

Orlando looked down, realizing for the first time that he was still holding on to her hand. Reluctantly he let it go, then looked up at her, trying to find a way to express the feelings that had overwhelmed him in the past few days. "Alicia," he said, with a catch in his throat. "My life . . . it's gotten real crazy all of a sudden. People are saying all kinds of things . . . things that just aren't true. If you heard anything that makes you doubt who I am or what I'm trying to do here—"

She reached out and put a finger to his lips to silence him. "I know who you are, Orlando Leone Jr.," she whispered. "And I know what you're trying to do. Don't ever doubt that." As Orlando breathed a sigh of pure relief, she smiled and continued, "And I know just what will take your mind off your troubles. A good home-cooked dinner."

"Dinner?" Orlando echoed, stunned that it was this beautiful and understanding woman who was offering him an invitation instead of the other way around.

She laughed at the blank look on his face. "You do eat dinner, don't you?" she asked with a gently teasing tone.

"Sure," Orlando replied, smiling back at her. "Dinner. Isn't that the thing that comes in a little box that you put in the microwave for three minutes?" He stood up. "I've got an idea that will cause you a lot less work," he continued. "Do you like Mexican food?"

"Qué bueno," she replied.

"Then I know a place you're going to love," he said, grabbing her coat off the chair and holding it up for her.

"You don't have—" she began.

He shook his head and opened the door for her with a flourish. "I insist," he interrupted. "It's the least I can do for a friend."

She blushed, a shade that matched the color in his own face, and arm in arm they made their way out onto the street where, as if by magic, a taxi was just then turning the corner. *Maybe this night is going to work out all right after all,* Orlando thought as he raised his hand to hail the cab.

Twenty minutes later, they were standing in the authentically decorated foyer of a fancy midtown restaurant as the hostess stared at Orlando with unabashed fascination. He turned and threw a rueful look to Alicia, and she knew that the cost of instant celebrity was more than this gentle and unassuming man was willing to pay. She cleared her throat and spoke directly to the ogling hostess. "A table for two," she said in a clear, firm voice. "And we'd prefer a booth in a quiet corner." The emphasis was hard to miss, and the hostess, suddenly embarrassed by her behavior, lowered her eyes and gathered up two menus.

"Right this way," she muttered.

Following her through the restaurant, they were intercepted by a short man in a flamboyant suit whom Orlando recognized as the manager of the establishment. "Mr. Leone?" he called out as he approached.

"Yes?" Orlando replied, suddenly dreading the encounter. All he wanted to do was to sit with Alicia and enjoy a couple of tacos.

Huffing and puffing like a steam engine, the manager stopped directly in front of him and proceeded to point his stubby forefinger at Orlando's chest to punctuate his words.

"You have disgraced the greatest fighter my country has ever had," he said in an outraged voice, "and you dare to set foot in my restaurant and expect to be served by my staff and eat my food?"

Orlando exchanged an exasperated look with Alicia. "Look," he said, turning to the manager, "I don't want any trouble. We're just—"

He stopped, dumbfounded, as the manager burst into a loud and sustained guffaw. Pulling out a large and colorful handkerchief from his pocket, he wiped sweat from his florid face and pounded Orlando on the back. "It is just my little joke, Mr. Leone," he wheezed. "I only joke with you."

He turned to the hostess. "Give Mr. Leone and his guest the best seats in the house," he commanded.

Turning back to Orlando, he continued in a confidential tone, "That Antonio Vasquez eats here every time he comes to our city. And let me tell you something . . . he is the worst tipper I have ever known! It is a shame to all Mexican people. He deserved to be humiliated by you, Señor Leone. You have taught him a lesson in false pride."

Alicia joined in the manager's laughter, but Orlando only sighed, unsure exactly how he felt about this jovial man's boisterous attempt at humor. Following the hostess to an intimate corner of the restaurant far removed from the other tables, Orlando glanced over at a five-piece mariachi band, immediately recognizing their familiar faces from the night before.

"Hey, guys," he called out, waving at them. "How's it going?"

The delighted musicians stopped in midnote and, rushing over, took turns shaking his hand and asking for autographs. The happy confusion drew the attention of the rest of the restaurant's patrons who broke into spontaneous applause when they realized that the latest front-page celebrity was actually in their midst. Even more chagrined now, Orlando smiled and waved back as he hurried Alicia along to their table and, he sincerely hoped, a little bit of precious privacy.

CHAPTER TWELVE

THE LIGHTS OF THE CITY RIPPLED ACROSS THE GENTLY flowing waters of the river, casting an enchanted glow beneath a canopy of stars on a clear and balmy evening along the broad promenade that ran along its banks. Older couples strolled hand in hand, and an occasional kid on a skateboard glided by. From the windows of the gracious old houses along the walk, soft golden light shone through the dappled leaves of trees, and somewhere, not far away, a street-corner musician played a lilting serenade.

Orlando and Alicia made their way slowly through the picturesque setting, in no hurry to be anywhere and savoring this moment for all its tranquillity and serenity. Both, in their silent thoughts, found themselves wishing this lovely boulevard could continue forever, leading them to nowhere in particular through a night that never ended.

"I'm sorry about the circus back there at the restaurant," Orlando said at last, breaking the comfortable silence they had held between them. "It really wasn't . . . ," he stammered, unsure of how much he could reveal of his true feelings, "you know . . . what I'd hoped for."

"And what had you hoped for?" was Alicia's equally tentative question.

Orlando took a deep breath. There was no other choice now but to plunge ahead. "I was just hoping to be able to spend some time with you. That's all."

She smiled. "Me too," she said simply, adding after a moment, "I'd like to get to know the man who's had such an effect on my daughter."

"Have I?" asked Orlando, genuinely surprised.

"Of course," Alicia responded. "She looks up to you so much." She lowered her eyes shyly. "And now I think I understand why." She looked up again, ready to take a few chances of her own. "Do you mind if I ask you a personal question?"

"Fire away," Orlando answered with a smile and stopped walking to face her directly.

"I've noticed that you're not wearing a wedding ring," she began, trying hard not to let her natural modesty get the best of her. She knew a respectable woman probably wouldn't be asking such questions, but right now all that mattered was his answer to her next query. "Does that mean you're still single?"

"No . . . ," Orlando began, stammering out his reply. "I mean, yes . . . I mean, I'm not married." He smiled, relieved to have gotten out a semicoherent response.

"Never?" Alicia persisted. And Orlando shook his head. "Engaged?" was her next question, and again a shake of his head gave her the answer she was hoping for. "What I don't understand," she continued after a moment, "is how a great guy like you wasn't nabbed by some lucky girl years ago."

Orlando shrugged, while in his mind he jubilantly repeated to himself that she had just called him a "great guy." "When I was a professional boxer," he explained, "all my time and energy went into my career. Then when I came back to serving God, I just naturally transferred my passions over to the work He had given me to do."

"All your passions?" Alicia asked softly.

Orlando thought for a moment. "I guess the answer to that would have to be both yes and no," he explained at last.

"I don't understand," Alicia replied, looking deeply into his eyes.

Orlando struggled to make his thoughts and feelings clear. "It's just that . . . I feel that God's brought me a long way in my life, but sometimes I find myself wishing, even praying, that He'll bring someone else along . . . someone who can share it with me. For almost forty years I've been on my own. I didn't intend for it to work out that way, but I guess the Lord had something else in mind. And then, one day not too long ago, it hit me, and it hit me hard."

"What did?" Alicia asked, never taking her eyes from his. "What hit you?"

"Just that," he said, swallowing hard, "I'm not indispensable to anyone." He sighed. "Oh, sure," he continued after a moment, "the kids at the center need me. But when it's all said and done, someone else could run the youth center. And the kids, they've got homes to go back to and parents who are trying to do the best they can. Most of them anyway."

He looked up into the starry sky, his thoughts, it seemed to her, a million miles away. "I always wished I had a family to come home to, someone who cared, my own children, people who I mattered to as a person." He turned back to her with a weary smile. "But, you know," he concluded, "God has given me the grace to endure . . . to stay focused on Him."

Alicia took a step closer to him. They were inches from each other, lost in the depth of each other's eyes. "Maybe God was just waiting for the right time," she said. "Maybe He was waiting to introduce you to the right person. Maybe that's what His grace is all about."

Suddenly Orlando reached out and pulled her close in a passionate yet firm embrace. He kissed her as if it were the only kiss he would ever give a woman. She fell into his arms as an Italian street-corner troubadour played his guitar and sang his song of love down the river walk. As they kissed, she felt a sudden conviction growing in her heart. God had meant for them to be together. He had ordained it from the beginning of time. She was His gift for a job well done.

The sound of buoy bells far off in the harbor still echoed in Orlando's mind the next morning as he stood watching a group of teens at the youth center playing a game of basketball. The night before seemed like a dream to him, or maybe today was the dream and he was still back at the river, walking arm in arm with a wonderful woman whom God seemed to have dropped into his life straight from heaven.

But harsh reality intruded when Orlando noticed a man with a television camera lurking at the edge of the court, shooting footage of him with a long-range lens. Orlando turned and walked back into the center.

"Hey, where are you going?" shouted one of the players. "We're about to mop the floor with these losers."

"Keep playing, guys," Orlando replied, noticing the disappointed look on the cameraman's face as he opened the door to the main hall. "You can give me the play-by-play later."

Inside, a harried mother with a determined look on her face accosted Orlando. "Mr. Leone, I've got to talk to you immediately," she demanded. Orlando inwardly groaned at what he knew was coming.

"Yes, Mrs. Haber?" he said politely.

"I've been hearing some very disturbing reports on the television," she said, launching into a well-rehearsed tirade. "They say that you're abusing the kids around here. Brainwashing them and all that. I'm here to tell you, Mr. Leone, that I, for one—"

"Imogene, what are you flapping your gums about?" came a voice behind Orlando, and he breathed a sigh of relief. His mother had come to the rescue and not a moment too soon. "Who are you going to trust—some airhead reporter babbling into a camera or a man who has, time and time again, proved that he will put the welfare of your children first?"

"But—" the flustered woman replied lamely.

"Don't you 'but' me," Geneva said, stepping in between her son and the hapless Mrs. Haber. "You've got one giant nerve coming over here and accusing my boy of anything whatsoever." She shook her finger in the now trembling woman's face. "You try that again, and I'll personally take my hand and slap you into next week."

"Mom, that's enough," Orlando said before Geneva swung around and pointed her long finger in his direction.

"And I don't want to hear any lip from you either!" she exclaimed as the woman beat a hasty retreat.

"Thanks for the help, Mom," Orlando said sarcastically, "but with that kind of approach we're going to end up in worse trouble than we are in now."

"What are you talking about, son?" Geneva asked, softening as she saw the worried look on his face.

Orlando shook his head. "With all this bad press, Mom," he explained, "our sponsors may start withdrawing their support from the center. Then I might as well give up trying to raise the money for the hospital."

"Give up?" repeated an outraged Geneva. "Give up? I never heard that kind of talk coming from you, Orlando." She held out her arms. "Come here, son," she said, giving him an enormous bear hug. "You and I have been in worse fights than this. We've got God on our side . . . and don't you forget it."

At that moment Darla ran up to Orlando and his mother, her black curly hair glistening in the morning sun and her dark eyes alight with excitement. "Mommy's coming!" she shouted excitedly, pointing to the front entrance. "Mommy's coming!"

The little girl's joy was infectious, and Orlando found himself sharing her laughter as he turned and saw Alicia coming toward them. "Excuse me, Mom," he said as he hurried up to meet Alicia, Darla close behind. Meeting in the middle of the room, the pair stopped in their tracks, each knowing what the other wanted, but not sure this was exactly the time and place to express the affection that was blossoming between them.

"I . . . uh . . . had some time between classes," Alicia explained. "I thought I'd come by, you know, to see how things were going."

Orlando smiled. "I'm glad you did," he said, before adding, "actually this place is turning into a real fishbowl. There are reporters and camera crews everywhere."

He looked at her as an idea began to dawn. "Hey," he said, his smile growing into a grin. "What do you say you and I go down to the park? It's a beautiful day, and if we're lucky, maybe no one will recognize me."

"I'd love to," answered Alicia, who was having a hard time keeping her eyes off him until she felt an insistent tugging at the hem of her dress.

"Can I go, too, Mommy?" Darla pleaded. "Please?"

Orlando and Alicia exchanged another glance, and both quickly dissolved into laughter. For the time being they were going to have to get used to having a little company. Orlando knelt down and put his hands on Darla's shoulders. "We wouldn't have it any other way," he told her.

The park was bustling with city dwellers seeking a few minutes of respite from the workaday world inside its leafy boundaries. Kite fliers, families with picnic baskets, and kids on bicycles dotted the broad meadow in the middle of the park, where Orlando and Alicia watched as Darla frolicked in the bright sunshine.

From a path meandering across the meadow a familiar figure approached. It was Kathleen, out for a morning jog. When Alicia caught sight of her old friend, she waved happily and cried out her name.

Kathleen stopped running and looked in Alicia's direction. She began to smile until she noticed the person her friend was standing with. Suddenly the happy expression faded, and turning on her heel, she deliberately began jogging off in the other direction.

Orlando couldn't help noticing the crestfallen expression on Alicia's face. "I guess I'm not too popular with your friend Kathleen," he remarked.

"It's not you," she replied. "I think it's God she's got a problem with."

Orlando sighed. "Not much I can do about that," he told her. "The Lord will have to deal with her in His own time . . . and His own way."

"That's what I'm afraid of," said Alicia, watching the retreating figure of her friend.

"I wouldn't worry too much," Orlando replied, trying to reassure her. "God knows just what He's doing, and if I was a betting man, I'd put my money on Him. Kathleen may be a handful, but the Lord specializes in hard cases." He smiled and pointed to himself. "I'm Exhibit A," he said.

A balloon vendor ambling by caught Darla's attention, and she ran back to Orlando and Alicia, clamoring for a handful of change to buy one of the bright floating spheres.

"I want a red one!" she proclaimed as the vendor stopped in front of them.

"Honey . . . ," Alicia began, but Orlando stepped forward, reaching into his pocket.

"Your best red balloon," he told the man, who smiled and sorted through his wares until he found the biggest and brightest of the lot. He handed it to Orlando, who passed it along to Darla with a courtly flourish. "One red balloon coming right up," he said with a bow and turned back to pay the vendor.

The delighted child grabbed the string and began skipping down the path, watching the bobbing shape above her dance against the blue sky. Suddenly a sparrow swooped low, causing the startled Darla to let go of the string. As the three of them watched, the balloon was whisked high into the sky.

"My balloon!" Darla cried.

"Sweetheart," Alicia gently scolded, "you need to be more careful and hang on tighter."

"That's okay," interjected Orlando. "It wasn't her fault."

"Yeah, Mommy," said Darla with childish defiance. "It wasn't my fault." She turned to Orlando. "Can I have another one?" she asked boldly.

"No," replied Alicia firmly. "One is enough for today." She looked at Orlando with mock severity. "Now don't go spoiling her," she warned him.

Orlando stooped down and put his arm around Darla, pointing up to the balloon already high above the city skyscrapers. "You know," he said, speaking to the child in a gentle, understanding voice, "when I was about your age, right after my daddy went to be with the Lord, my mom and I would come to this very park every once in a while. And sometimes she'd buy me a balloon too. Then at the end of the day, we'd let that balloon go free."

"Why?" asked the wide-eyed Darla. "Didn't you like it anymore?"

"I loved those balloons," Orlando explained. "But, you see, my mom told me that my dad, up in heaven, would like to have a balloon too. So we'd go ahead and send it up to him." He followed the little girl's gaze to the speck of red overhead.

"Maybe my balloon will go to your daddy too," Darla said.

"I hope so, sweetheart," replied Orlando. "But in the meantime, if you want another balloon, I'd be happy to get one for you."

Darla looked hopefully to her mother, who smiled and nodded her approval. "When I'm finished playing, I'm going to let my new balloon go too," she told them. "For Bugsy."

"Who's Bugsy?" asked Orlando.

Alicia slipped her arm through his. "He was a cocker spaniel," she explained. "He died last year. Darla says a prayer for him almost every night." Then together, the man, the woman, and the child turned to look up into the sky just as the red balloon vanished from sight.

CHAPTER THIRTEEN

On a videotape replay, Antonio Vasquez laid into his sparring partner with a vengeance, hammering at his midsection with a vicious rain of rapid punches that left his opponent dazed and breathless. Ruthlessly pursuing his advantage, the champion landed several roundhouse rights to the head, sending the other boxer crashing to the floor with a spray of blood and sweat.

Freddie and Sam Freeman sat in the lavish living room of the boxing promoter's country estate watching the heavyweight finish up the merciless assault on a big-screen television. "Ever since that run-in with the security guard," Freddie observed, "the champ has really been acting like he's got something to prove."

Freeman nodded in agreement. "He's doubled his workout time," he commented. "I've never seen him so driven. It's like he's got a demon in him or something."

"He was starting to get a little fat and sassy," Freddie remarked with a shrug. "Maybe that fight at the hotel was the best thing that could have happened to him."

"For more reasons than one," replied Freeman.

"What do you mean by that?" Freddie asked with a nervous flutter in his voice.

"Simple," said Freeman. "We stage a rematch. We get this security guard to get into the ring with the champ. It's a publicity bonanza and a perfect setup for your next legitimate match."

Freddie, his hands moving quickly as he lit a cigarette, shook his head. "I don't think so, boss," he said with a firmness in his voice. "I . . . I don't think this guy would do it."

"What?" demanded Freeman. "You can read his mind all of a sudden?" He stood up and, tapping Freddie on the top of his head, began to pace the room. "Don't be stupid, Freddie. There's not a man in the world that can't be bought. We give him a million dollars, and we make twenty or more. He takes his punishment like a man, then we get the champ back in the headlines. What could be simpler?"

"You don't know these religious types," Freddie insisted, puffing rapidly on his cigarette. "It's not about the money for them." He crushed the cigarette in a crystal ashtray. "It's never about the money," he added bitterly.

"It's *always* about the money," was Freeman's sarcastic reply.

Freddie seemed desperate now, trying to win an argument as if he were competing in a sporting event. "No," he insisted. "You can't just pay this guy off. He's got this ministry thing. It's like he's all wrapped up in trying to get to heaven or something." He gestured toward the television. "You saw him," he said. "He's got that look in his eyes. Besides," he added with a nervous laugh, "he's an old man. There's no fight left in him."

Freeman stopped pacing and fixed Freddie with a penetrating look. "Whose side are you on in this thing anyway?" he demanded to know. "If I didn't know better, I'd swear you were going soft or something."

"It's not that, Mr. Freeman," Freddie said defensively. "It's just—"

"It's just that Antonio's reputation is being ruined by this nobody," interrupted Freeman. "He's got to redeem his good name. We can't have people going around saying the heavyweight champion of the world was taken down by some forty-year-old security guard who sucker punched him."

"There was nothing official about what happened in that hotel room," Freddie insisted, sweat beginning to bead up on his forehead. "He's still the champ, and this guy is still just some has-been fighter. This whole thing's going to blow over. You'll see."

"Don't you get it?" sneered Freeman. "This isn't about what's official or not. It's all about the public perception of the champ. He's got to be seen as the best there is, with no exceptions. Besides, this is just the kind of concept the press is going to eat up. We'll make a fortune on the pay-per-view rights alone. There's a big payday in all of this, so I don't want to hear any more negative thinking, you got that?"

"Yes, Mr. Freeman," Freddie said sullenly. A long moment of silence passed.

"So?" said Freeman, impatiently looking at his watch. "What are you waiting for?"

Freddie looked at him incredulously. "Me?" he said. "You want me to put this together? But—"

"You already blew one job for me," Freeman said in a tone that sent a chill down Freddie's spine. "You better make sure this one goes off without a hitch."

"Wha . . . what are you talking about?" Freddie sputtered.

Freeman took a step toward him, his eyes glittering with menace. "Remember that little collection job I sent you out on?"

"You mean . . . Michael?" Freddie asked, swallowing hard.

"Yeah, Michael," Freeman answered. "Well, guess what? The gravity lesson you tried to teach him didn't stick."

"What do you mean?" Freddie asked, his skin the color of the white carpet beneath his feet.

"I mean he lived. In fact, not only did he live," Freeman growled, "he's in the hospital right now and expected to make a full recovery. And when he gets out, the Feds will be right there, ready to take his testimony for an indictment against me."

"But, Mr. Freeman," Freddie said, his voice cracking, "that was a six-story drop. No one could have survived—"

Freeman lunged at him, grabbing him by the collar and shaking him hard as he screamed, "Are you trying to tell me there's not a guy in a guarded room in St. Francis getting ready to spill everything he knows about our operation? Is that what you're trying to tell me, Freddie?"

"No . . . no, sir," stammered the shocked Freddie.

Freeman let him go, straightening his tie and shooting his cuffs. "Good," he said, his voice returning to a conversational tone. He leaned over and patted Freddie on the cheek, a little too hard. "Very good, Freddie," he purred. "So I guess you'd better get busy with your life-and-death assignment."

"Life and death?" Freddie whispered hoarsely.

"That's right," replied Freeman. "You've got to make this fight live. Or something else will die."

Freddie stood up, the wheels of his mind spinning frantically. "Don't worry, Mr. Freeman," he said, regaining his confidence and self-assurance. "I'll fix it. I'll make this happen, guaranteed."

"I'd be very interested to hear what you've got in mind, since there's so much at stake for you," his boss replied.

Freddie slipped on his coat and looked at his watch. "All in good time, Mr. Freeman," he said. "Right now, I need a hundred thousand in cash, no questions asked. Actually, *you* need a hundred thousand in cash. I'll explain it all later. I need you to do something to set this all in motion."

Without blinking, Freeman walked to one of the dark and disturbing abstract paintings on the wall and, moving it open on a hinge, revealed a wall safe. Deftly spinning the lock back and forth, he opened it. Then he pulled out several packets of crisp new bills and turned back to Freddie.

"You better know what you're doing," Freeman snarled.

"I do, believe me," he said. "One more thing, Mr. Freeman."

"Yeah?" asked Freeman. "What is it?"

"When I put this all together for you, we're not just even. We're paid up in full. Deal?"

Freeman glared at him for a moment, silently calculating the odds of eliminating Freddie here and now. *No,* he thought, *let's see what he's got up his sleeve.* "Deal," he said in a low voice that carried with it an unspoken understanding that he was willing to lose his number one enforcer if it came to that.

Freddie explained the "assignment" he wanted his boss to carry out step-by-step, insisting that he follow the instructions to a T. Reluctantly, Freeman went along with it. Freddie then stood, put on his dark wraparound sunglasses, and as he left said, "Remember, let me know as soon as you've got it." Freddie hustled outside, hopped into his sleek black Lexus, and sped away.

Two hours later, Freeman's limo pulled into the gravel driveway of a seedy mobile home park on the outskirts of the city. The limo pulled to a stop, and Freeman got out, alone. Mangy dogs lounged in the shade, and laundry hung from sagging lines strung between the rusty and peeling trailers. Checking the addresses on the mailboxes, he located the object of his search at the rear of the park behind the wrecked carcasses of several old trucks and cars. Careful to keep his polished shoes out of the dust and debris that littered the front yard, he walked to the screen door and rapped loudly on it with the knuckle of his forefinger.

"Hello?" he called out. "Anyone home?"

A long moment passed as a shuffling sound announced the slow approach of the mobile home's resident. From behind the screen door, the ravaged face of an elderly woman appeared. Her hair covered in a ratty knit cap and her hunched body wrapped in a faded housecoat, she looked suspiciously at the stranger standing at her door.

"Are you Martha Stallings?" asked Freeman pleasantly.

"Who wants to know?" she asked between toothless gums.

"I knew your husband," he explained. "Gabby Stallings. He was a great trainer, Mrs. Stallings. One of the best in the whole sport of boxing."

The woman's face softened at the mention of her late husband's name. "Who are you?" she asked in a friendlier tone.

"Sam Freeman's the name," he replied and smiled. "Gabby and I worked together in the fight game years ago. Do you mind if I come in?" He looked up into the sky. "Looks like it might start raining soon."

The woman swung open the screen door, letting out several yowling cats in the process. Freeman stepped into the dim light of the mobile home, his eyes taking a moment to adjust to the shadows where a lifetime of debris and useless mementos had piled to the ceiling. *The place is a dump,* Freeman thought as he smiled at his hostess. He hoped she could find what he was looking for in this garbage dump.

"I don't get much company," said Martha Stallings, sweeping a stack of old magazines to the floor to clear a space on a faded sofa for Freeman to sit. "I can't offer you nothing to drink," she continued. "My check is late this month."

"Please don't trouble yourself," he said smoothly, taking the seat and leaning forward to engage the woman eye to eye. "Martha—may I call you Martha?—I understand Gabby passed away a few years ago."

The woman's eyes glistened with tears. "Two years next month," she said sadly. "There isn't a day that passes—"

"Yes, it's very sad," interrupted Freeman, trying to get to the point of his visit. He had to move swiftly and didn't have time for some old woman's rambling memories. "I've been told that your husband was the trainer of a young fighter named Orlando Leone Jr. He was the cruiserweight champion about ten years ago. Do you remember?"

The woman tapped her temple with one finger. "I'm not as senile as I look," she said. "I remember like it was yesterday. Gabby trained him and Orlando's brother, Alfredo Leone, managed him. They had a contract. Eight fights. But only seven were completed. I remember because Gabby always used to say how he wished he could have seen Leone get into the ring just one more time. He said he was a contender, a real contender. He could have gone all the way to the heavyweight championship."

Pay dirt! thought Freeman. *Now all that is left to do is finesse this old woman for a few more minutes and then get out of this rat hole as fast as I can.* "That's absolutely right, Mrs. Stallings," Freeman said smoothly. "No flies on you, eh?" He laughed, then leaned in even closer and said, "Mrs. Stallings, you may be interested to know that I represent the business interests of Mr. Orlando Leone Jr. As his attorney and adviser, I've become aware of some contractual complications that have arisen out of his failure to complete the terms of the agreement he had with your husband."

"What kind of complications?" asked the woman, suddenly suspicious again. She narrowed her eyes at Freeman, the creaky gears of her mind trying to work out what this slick stranger was after.

"You don't need to concern yourself with that and, besides, attorney-client privilege doesn't allow me to disclose it," he said, reaching over and patting her on the arm. "Let me get right to the point, Mrs. Stallings"—he tried to hide his smirk—"since I know your time is very valuable. Mr. Leone is now engaged in helping inner-city youth to find new hope and direction. Isn't that wonderful?"

"I heard about that," replied the woman. "Gabby always said as much as Leone should have kept fighting, he always admired his decision to give it all up to help other people. That's why he never held him to that last fight in the contract. It didn't seem right to him."

"Of course not," continued Freeman, moving in for the kill. "But, you see, the situation has now changed somewhat. The fact is, in order for Mr. Leone to continue his good work among the youth of our city, it is necessary for him to buy the half of the contract that your husband held."

"But why?" asked Mrs. Stallings, trying hard to stay ahead of these confusing developments.

"As I say," Freeman repeated, trying to hide his annoyance, "you needn't bother yourself with that. It's a private legal matter." He looked around the dingy room. "I understand Mr. Stallings was not exactly a wealthy man when he passed away. It must be difficult for you to get by on just your social security check."

"You've got that right," exclaimed the woman.

"Well, then," continued Freeman, "you're going to be very happy to hear what I have to tell you."

"Yes?" she said, suddenly all ears.

"You see," said Freeman, "Mr. Leone has authorized me to undertake the purchase of your husband's 50 percent share of the contract from his legal heir, which is you, for the sum of one hundred thousand dollars." He reached into his suit pocket and produced the packets of bills, laying them with a flourish on the coffee table. "Mr. Leone hopes that this will help ease your grief at the passing of your husband and help you to be more comfortable during your twilight years."

The woman's eyes looked as if they were ready to pop completely out of her head. She picked up one of the bundles of bills and flipped through it, listening to the soft rustle of the paper between her fingers. "Orlando would do this," she said in a whisper, "for me?" Now tears began to flow in earnest. "God bless him! And God bless you."

"That's not necessary. What's important now is that we reach an agreement regarding the contract so that Orlando can move on with his work in the ministry." He stuck out his hand. "Do we have a deal, Mrs. Stallings?"

She looked at his hand, then back at the bills, then over at Freeman's smiling face. "You know," she said, "I have only Gabby's half of the contract. The other half is still owned by Mr. Leone's brother. Have you been in contact with him? You know, he was very upset when Orlando quit fighting. I don't think he ever forgave him."

"Don't you worry your head about that," Freeman replied. "I'm sure Mr. Alfredo Leone will be only too happy to cooperate if it means his brother will be able to continue his good works." He stuck his hand out farther, almost under the woman's nose. "Deal?" he repeated.

A wide grin grew on Martha Stallings's wrinkled face. Taking Freeman's hand, she shook it vigorously with a surprisingly strong grip. "Deal," she replied and, gathering up the money, began squirreling it away in the pockets of her housecoat.

"So," Freeman said, delivering the final stroke, "where would that contract be?"

Mrs. Stallings looked at him as if she were about to share an earth-shattering secret. "I keep all my important papers under my mattress," she explained. "I never trust those banks with their fancy safety-deposit boxes. Nothing safe about them, if you ask me."

"Don't you worry, Mrs. Stallings," Freeman said as he followed her into the back bedroom. "That contract is going to be perfectly safe in my hands."

Before long Freeman legally owned 50 percent of an old fight contract that, for all he knew, could be worthless. How was Freddie going to pull off the rest? How was he going to find this elusive, angry brother, Alfredo, who had been gone for ten years? Or was Freddie just buying time until he could skip town and go underground to save his neck? Only time would tell. But time was running out and getting very expensive.

CHAPTER FOURTEEN

ALICIA WAS CONCENTRATING COMPLETELY ON THE MASS OF clay set before her on the workbench. Above her, pinned to the wall, was a picture of Orlando's father, Orlando Sr. Even as she worked, she marveled again at how much of the strong character reflected in the father's face had been passed down to the son.

After finishing the rough model of the bust she had been commissioned to do for the youth center, Alicia spent several weeks studying the face as she prepared to begin work on the final product. She felt that she knew the lines of the man's face by heart and that, from her heart, the knowledge could flow at last through her fingers and into the shape of the clay. It was how she had always worked, creating a sculpture from the inside out, from her own deep understanding of the human physique and the truth revealed in every face. Good or bad, it was there to read if only you had the eyes to see.

Molding the clay with wet hands, she began the preliminary shaping when a noise behind her interrupted her work. She turned to see Darla rushing toward her with outstretched arms, and teasing the little girl, she held up her clay-covered hands like a movie monster about to attack. Darla stopped dead in her tracks and screamed with childish delight. She turned to Orlando, who was standing in the doorway with a strange expression of expectancy on his face.

"My mommy's playing in the mud!" Darla said with a laugh.

"It's clay, sweetheart," her mother corrected her and, noticing the look on Orlando's face, turned to him. "Is everything okay?" she asked.

"It's fine," he said, crossing the room to give her a check. "It's just that . . . well . . ." He couldn't seem to get his words out.

"What is it, Orlando?" she asked, standing up and wiping her hands clean with a towel. ·

"Listen," he said after a moment's pause, "I know you're busy right now, but how about you and me going someplace together."

"Where?" she asked.

"It's kind of a surprise," he replied.

Darla clapped her hands together. "I love surprises!" she exclaimed.

Orlando knelt down next to her. "Darla," he said, looking her straight in the eye, "this is kind of a special surprise. Just for your mom." He gave her a hug. "I'll tell you what," he continued. "How about we drop you off at the youth center and you can practice your singing for Aunt Geneva? Then later we can all go out to dinner together."

"Okay," said Darla agreeably. "That'll be fun."

"You're being very mysterious," remarked Alicia, cocking her head to one side as she regarded the man she had, over these past few weeks, come to love and respect.

"Will you come?" That was all Orlando would say, and the pleading look in his eyes told her how important it was to him.

"Let me get my coat," she said.

A half hour later, Orlando was leading her up the steps of an old but well-tended apartment building in a section of the city that had managed to keep the ravages of poverty, gangs, and drugs at bay. They rang the bell, and a buzzer let them into a freshly painted lobby where a clean-swept stairway led to the upper stories.

"Where are we?" Alicia asked persistently.

"Just at the top of the stairs," Orlando urged her. "Then you'll see."

They arrived at an apartment door on the fourth floor, which opened at Orlando's knock. Alicia was surprised to find that they had arrived at the home of Simon, the pastor from the youth center.

Simon, for his part, seemed as surprised to see them as she was to see him. "Well, well," he said, his face breaking into a wide smile as he showed them in. "To what do I owe this very special and, I might add, unexpected pleasure?"

Orlando, who hadn't been able to shake his sense of nervous expectation since arriving at Alicia's studio, cleared his throat. "Simon," he said, and the pastor and Alicia exchanged a quick look when they heard the trembling tone of his voice. *What is wrong with this man?* they asked each other wordlessly. "How long has it been since you performed a wedding ceremony?"

Alicia's heart skipped a beat when she heard those words. "Orlando," she asked, "what's going on here?"

He held her off with a wave of his hand, focusing his attention on Simon. "Well," he repeated, "how long?"

"My, my," said Simon, scratching his white chin whiskers, "it has to have been at least ten or twelve years now." He looked from one of his guests to the other. "But something tells me I'm about to be performing another one pretty soon."

Alicia held up her hands. "Don't look at me," she said. "I don't know any more about this than you do." She turned to Orlando. "Please," she said. "The suspense is killing me."

"Amen to that," echoed Simon.

Orlando turned to face Alicia directly, taking her hands in his. "Alicia," he began, but before he could get another word out, he seemed to lose himself in her eyes.

"Yes?" Alicia prompted, her heart pounding wildly.

"Alicia," he began again. "It says in the Bible that it's better to marry than to burn. Now I'm not saying I'm burning . . . But I do believe I'm starting to smell some smoke."

Alicia could not break away from Orlando's stare any more than she could have freed herself from earth's gravitational pull. "Orlando, please," she whispered. "I've been through enough in my life to have learned not to take anything for granted." She smiled encouragingly. "Maybe it would be best if you just spelled it out for me . . . in plain English."

Dropping to one knee, Orlando looked up at her as if she might have been an angel descending on clouds of glory. "Alicia," he said, his voice strong and clear now, "I love you with all my heart. I've loved you since the moment I laid eyes on you. The truth is, I don't think I can live without you." Letting go of one of her hands for a moment, he reached into the breast pocket of his shirt and pulled out a simple gold band. "Will you marry me?" he said.

Alicia caught her breath and held it. The room was so quiet that the sound of Simon's grandfather clock thundered like Big Ben.

"Because if you don't," Orlando continued without giving her a chance to answer, "I'll be the most miserable and lonely man on this whole planet. I'll probably shut myself away from contact with another living soul for the rest of my natural life. I'll never stop thinking about you. I'll call out your name every morning and every night until my throat is raw and I can't—"

"Stop!" Alicia cried, laughing with delight and joy. "I think I've got the picture." She drew him up from his knees and looked him straight in the eye. "Yes, Mr. Orlando Leone, your life is saved," she pronounced concisely. "I would be honored to become your wife."

"My, my," Simon mused as the two fell into each other's arms for a long and lingering kiss. "God sure is grand, bringing you two together from the ends of the earth. I should say so!" It was only a moment later that he realized he might just as well have been talking to himself for all the attention his guests were paying him.

Two weeks later, Alicia's studio was a bustle of colorful activity as a gaggle of volunteers decorated the room in anticipation of the afternoon's reception. Tables set up in the large studio space were draped in pure white linen with a beautiful floral centerpiece on each one. Bunting hung from the walls, and the ceiling was clustered with scores of multicolored balloons. The doorways were bordered with entwined roses and ribbons, and the mariachi band from the Mexican restaurant was practicing its set.

In the midst of all the confusion stood Geneva, shouting orders, sending scurrying children off on various errands, and generally whipping the wedding into shape with the skill and authority of a veteran drill sergeant. It was only when she saw Orlando enter the room, carrying his wedding tux in a plastic dry cleaning bag over his shoulder, that she stopped her campaign to have everything perfect and hurried over to her son.

"How are you feeling, Orlando?" she asked him after giving her son a tight and warm hug.

"How am I supposed to feel?" Orlando asked. "Like my stomach and my brain have switched places."

She patted him on the arm. "Everything's going to be just fine," she said, casting an eagle eye around the room for any signs of slacking off. Then taking him aside, she pulled him close to her and whispered in his ear. "I have a surprise for you, Orlando," she told him.

"Please, Mom," Orlando groaned. "I'm nervous enough as it is."

"I think you're going to like this," she replied, then smiled teasingly. "Of course, if you'd rather not know—"

"Come on, Mom," said Orlando. "I'm in no mood for games. Just spill it, okay?"

Geneva's eyes twinkled. "Of all the people you would want to see you get married, who would be at the top of your list?" she asked.

"What is this?" an exasperated Orlando said with a sigh. "Some kind of guessing game?"

"Just answer the question, son," Geneva replied sternly.

Orlando thought a moment. "I'd have to say I wish Dad were here today," he ventured after a moment.

His mother looked at him with love in her eyes. "Me, too, son," she said softly. "I know he would be so proud." She leaned over to kiss him. "I can't bring him back," she continued, "but maybe I can do the next best thing."

"Which is . . . ?" Orlando asked.

"You better go get ready, or you'll be late. I'll tell you later," Geneva said.

Orlando's face lit with exuberant curiosity. "C'mon, Ma!" he shouted. But then a shadow of doubt passed over his eyes. "Is it somebody I really need to see?"

Geneva laughed. "Don't you worry," she told her son. "He said he'd think about it. If he shows, there'll be no mistake about who it is."

Every woman, Alicia knew, dreams of the perfect wedding— the one day that belongs just to her, when all the hope and joy and best wishes of the whole world seem to be hers alone and the future looks bright with a lifetime partner to share it. Even though the little chapel where the ceremony was held wasn't the grand cathedral of her childhood fantasies, even though the bridesmaids were a slightly offbeat collection of her sculpting students and a few kids from the center, even though the dress she wore was borrowed from Orlando's mother and the ring around her finger was not set with the largest sparkling diamond—none of that seemed to matter. The ceremony of Alicia Corbin and Orlando Leone Jr. was witnessed by the most important and prestigious guest any wedding could ever hope to have. Alicia knew it the minute she stepped foot on the long carpeted aisle that led to the small altar where Simon, in his Sunday-best pastor suit, was waiting. She could feel God's Spirit hovering in the room like the brush of angels' wings, and she could feel His presence touch and transform every person in the small sanctuary.

Pomp and circumstance would only have detracted from the true glory that was present to hear and to bless the marriage vows they exchanged—the glory of the Lord that had brought them together and would give unbreakable strength to their bond. The wedding had been perfect, and as Alicia took the name Leone as her own, she couldn't help offering up a small but intensely heartfelt prayer to the One who had made the dream come true for her.

The same aura of heavenly visitation followed them back to her studio where the reception was a chance for the two sides of the new family to meet and greet one another. More of Alicia's students, past and present, had turned out for the occasion, along with alumni from the youth center and even a few of Orlando's old boxing cronies. The mariachi band proved its versatility by seamlessly shifting from Mexican dance music to romantic Italian ballads and even a few polkas and waltzes for the older guests. One of Alicia's most creative students, who had an interest in both sculpture and photography, did the honor of snapping pictures for a wedding album, and Geneva stood at the buffet table making sure there was plenty of good old-fashioned Italian pasta for everyone to enjoy. *Only one thing is missing,* Alicia thought sadly as she looked over the throng of people. Kathleen wasn't there to share her joy.

Still dressed in their wedding clothes, Orlando and Alicia greeted their guests, posed for snapshots, and shared a dance with anyone and everyone who wanted to take a spin across the floor. It was late afternoon before they were finally able to sit down and have a bite of Geneva's mouthwatering lasagna. But before Orlando could raise a fork to his mouth, he caught sight of a figure across the room that made him freeze, hardly daring to breathe for fear that the image would fade and he would discover it was all a dream.

"What is it, darling?" asked Alicia, who had noticed her husband's sudden stiffness.

Orlando set down his fork and stood up. "Excuse me a minute, would you, Alicia?" he asked and, without looking at her, began to cross the crowded room.

"Don't worry, honey," a voice behind her said, and she felt Geneva's reassuring touch on her shoulder. "It's just that Orlando hasn't seen his brother in so many years."

Crossing the room as if in a daze, Orlando couldn't help but call out, "Alfredo! Alfredo! You big bum, I can't believe you came." In an instant, the two brothers were in each other's arms, locked in a bear hug that seemed to close the distances of time and memory that had separated them for so long. Unbelievable as it may seem, Freddie, the ruthless enforcer for Sam Freeman, was also Alfredo, Orlando's long lost brother. Alfredo hung on the tightest and the longest, overwhelmed by the sudden feelings that had welled up and not willing to look his brother in the eye until he could pull himself together.

"I just can't believe you actually showed up," said Orlando when at last they stood face-to-face.

"Wouldn't have missed it," his brother answered. "Like I told Mom, we're family." He reached out and mussed Orlando's hair. "It's great to see you, kid," he said, and in that moment he was surprised to hear in his own tone of voice that he actually meant it. "It's been too long." He shrugged and laughed. "Except that you keep showing up on television every five minutes."

Orlando laughed. "It's driving me crazy," he admitted, then faked a punch to his brother's midsection. "So how are you? What have you been up to? Are you married? Do you have any kids?"

"Whoa," Alfredo said, holding up his hands. "One question at a time."

"You can fill me in later," Orlando responded, grabbing his brother by the arm. "Right now I want you to meet Alicia."

Hurrying him across the room, Orlando could see Alicia rising from her chair to greet them, a broad smile on her radiant face. "Alicia," he said when they arrived at the table, "this is my brother, Alfredo, but everybody calls him Freddie—except me and Mom. Alfredo, this is my wife, Alicia."

"It's a pleasure to finally meet you, Freddie," Alicia said, shaking his hand. "I've heard so much about you."

"Don't believe everything you hear, Alicia," he said in mock warning, and the three of them laughed as if they were old and dear friends. At that moment, Darla skipped up to them. She was wearing an adorable flower-print bridesmaid gown and had tiny white flowers woven into her hair.

"Darla," Alicia said, lifting the child in her arms. "I'd like you to meet your new uncle, Freddie."

"Hello, Uncle Freddie," said Darla. "Do you want to dance with me?"

Freddie bowed low. "It would be my pleasure to share a dance with the newest and most beautiful member of the Leone family," he said and, taking her from Alicia's arms, whisked her onto the floor.

The rest of the reception seemed to pass by in a happy blur for the newlyweds as the afternoon turned to evening and the music played on. Finally, as the excitement and laughter died down, Orlando and Alicia took to the floor alone to dance a graceful waltz, and the guests watched in silent approval of such a blessed and beautiful couple. As the dance ended and applause echoed through the room, Geneva marched determinedly to the middle of the floor and held up her hands for silence. The room was immediately quiet. No one, it seemed, would dare to disobey the mistress of ceremonies for the day's events.

"Ladies and gentlemen," she announced to the assembled crowd, "in honor of my new daughter-in-law"—her eyes twinkled—"not to mention my new grandchild, we have a very special treat for you all coming up. They say that music is the way God speaks to His people about the beauty of His creation, and the music you're about to hear is surely some of the sweetest in all of God's creation." She clapped her hands. "Okay, kids," she commanded. "Let's get it on."

One by one the members of the youth center choir emerged from the throng and came together in neat rows in the middle of the dance floor. With all eyes on Geneva they waited patiently for their cue and then began the soft and gentle words and melody of "'Tis So Sweet." Before long, nearly everyone in the room had joined in singing the timeless hymn, and those who didn't know the words closed their eyes and let the music carry them away.

For Freddie, however, the grace and blessing of the gathered voices seemed to stir deep and uncontrollable emotions inside him. Choking back the unfamiliar sensation of tears, he slipped out of the hall and into the night. As he did, the stately gospel hymn suddenly was transformed into a rollicking hip-hop beat as the choir performed a dance routine that brought people to their feet.

It was shortly before midnight when the guests gathered outside, ready to pelt the newlyweds with rice as they ran to the taxi on their way to a short honeymoon before Orlando had to return to his busy schedule and Alicia resumed her teaching duties. Upstairs, Geneva held Darla in her arms while Alicia did some last-minute packing.

"The cab is here," Orlando announced, walking into the bedroom. Catching a glimpse of Darla's sorrowful expression, he nodded to Alicia, who stopped what she was doing and went to comfort her daughter.

"Now, honey," she said gently. "Please don't be sad. We'll be gone only seven days. Can you count seven on your fingers?" Solemnly Darla held up her small hands and numbered seven fingers. "That's all," said Alicia. "Then we'll be back. And in the meantime, you and Grandma Geneva are going to have a wonderful time."

"Will you bring me back a present?" the little girl asked, a smile beginning to spread across her face.

"Of course we will, sweetheart," Orlando said as he picked up the suitcases. "That's a promise."

Darla hugged them both, then went happily back into Geneva's arms.

"Now," Alicia said sternly, "don't go spoiling her, Geneva."

"That's a grandmother's privilege," Geneva snapped back and gave her granddaughter a hug. "Isn't it, honey bunch?"

Hurrying downstairs, Orlando and Alicia ran the gauntlet of rice and well wishes and then climbed into the back of a taxi taking them to the airport. Pulling away from the familiar street, Alicia looked back and asked wistfully, "Do you think Darla's going to be all right?"

"I'd be surprised if you can pry her away from my mother by the time we get back," Orlando replied. He put his arm around her shoulder and pulled her close to him. "Don't you worry about a thing," he said. "This next week is going to be our time. To me, all that exists is you."

They rode in silence for a while until Alicia looked up at her husband and said, "It was wonderful having your brother come today. I don't know him very well, but he seemed troubled about something."

"He was probably just a little uncomfortable," Orlando ventured. "He's been away from the family for so long."

"Maybe," mused Alicia, "but it seemed to me that he was thinking about something else . . . as if his mind were in another room." She settled back against Orlando's shoulder. "I'm sure it'll be fine," she sighed contentedly, "once I get to know him better."

On the expressway now, the taxi maneuvered around a momentary slowdown of traffic, speeding up as it switched to the passing lane and overtook a black Lexus. At the wheel, Freddie smoked a cigarette and stared out across the city skyline, thinking back on all the questions his brother had asked him at the moment they saw each other again. *Are you married? Do you have kids?* Freddie sighed. Tonight, it was enough to still be breathing. Who knew what tomorrow might bring?

CHAPTER FIFTEEN

"WELL, WELL, WELL," SIMON EXCLAIMED, WINKING AS HE smiled. "Someone certainly does have that extra spring in his step this morning."

Orlando laughed and clapped the older man on the back. "I guess it shows, doesn't it?" he said with a grin that would do justice to a cat who'd just eaten the canary.

"Oh, my, yes," replied the pastor. "There's nothing in the world like the shine on the face of a happily married man."

It was a week to the day after Alicia and Orlando had left for their honeymoon. Coming back, it had seemed to them that, while nothing had really changed, everything had changed. Work was still waiting for them, the daily routine that taxed their energies and utilized their skills and abilities to the maximum. Now it seemed to be for a reason. With each having the other, a new purpose had been born, a point in carrying on, a fresh direction for the future.

But Orlando barely had time to enjoy this strange yet satisfying sensation, waving to some kids at the court and checking the pile of mail that waited for him on his desk, before his mother burst in. He could immediately tell from the look on her face that something was wrong—very wrong.

"It's good to have you back, son," she said, giving him a distracted peck on the cheek. "I don't know how we manage around here without you."

"Mom," he replied, looking her straight in the eye, "let's cut the small talk, okay? What's going on? I can tell just by looking at you . . . you can't hide it from me."

She stared back at him, tears glistening in the corners of her eyes. "I think you better hear it from Pete," she said. "He's got all the details down better than I do."

"Where is he then?" Orlando wanted to know.

As if on cue, his lawyer walked through the office door, carrying a briefcase bulging with legal papers. "Welcome back, Orlando," he said mournfully, taking a seat at the desk. "But when you hear what I've got to tell you, you may wish you'd stayed away."

"Just give it to me straight," replied Orlando, also taking a seat. *Why can't I just live a normal life?* he thought as he tried to brace for the bad news. *Why is God always testing my strength and trying my faith?*

"I got a call from Jerry and Patricia Bowman this morning," Pete began. "They are withdrawing their support from the center. In fact, they're demanding to be reimbursed for all the money they've contributed this year."

"What?" shouted an outraged Orlando. "The Bowmans have been donors since we started this place. I can't believe they'd do this, especially now, when we're trying to get the hospital remodeling started."

"It's those crazy headlines in the newspapers," Geneva explained. "All that talk about brainwashing children and being a cult leader. It just scared them off, son."

"And I've got a feeling they're not the only ones," added Pete.

"I've seen this kind of thing happen before. One donor drops out, and it starts a chain reaction. They start acting like a herd of sheep, all running scared in the same direction."

Geneva nodded. "When you get older, you get a little scared sometimes."

"Scared?" Pete snorted. "They got downright paranoid. They must have told me they'd rather be safe than sorry a dozen times."

"Maybe if I just talked to them," Orlando conjectured desperately.

Pete shook his head. "Too late for that," he said. "They've already given the money to another charity."

"Just like that?" asked Orlando bitterly. "They didn't even bother to get my side of the story."

"Hey," countered Pete, "it's not like they were under contract with us or anything. They can put their money anywhere they want to, and there's not a thing we can do about it."

"I've got to try to change their minds," Orlando said, as much to himself as to the other people in the office. "We've got to finance that construction loan. If we don't, they postpone the whole building process."

"That's not all," continued Pete in a low voice.

Orlando groaned. "Isn't that enough? I don't think I can handle any more bad news, especially now, only a day back from my honeymoon."

"The honeymoon is over," Pete said, trying to hide his compassion for his friend behind a gruff exterior. "This one is really going to rock your world."

"I'm afraid to ask," said Orlando.

"I'm afraid to tell you," replied Pete, "but as your attorney and your friend, I've got no choice." He took a deep breath.

"I got a call this morning from a representative of Antonio Vasquez."

"The boxing champion?" asked a puzzled Geneva.

"That's the one," replied Pete, nodding grimly. "Apparently," he continued, turning to Orlando, "they want to fight again. Only this time, it's not going to be in some hotel room."

Orlando stared at him incredulously, then began to laugh, letting out all the tension and disappointment of the past few minutes in a gale of hilarity. "Let me get this straight," he said at last, after catching his breath. "The heavyweight champion of the world wants to get into the ring with me? Why? What's that going to prove?" Before Pete could answer, Orlando added, "I have no interest in fighting anyone for any price. I'm thirty-nine years old. My life is not even close to being what it was. This is nonsense."

"Maybe to you, it is. But think about it from Vasquez's point of view," replied Pete, leaning forward in his chair. "You humiliated him in front of the entire country. How is he ever going to get his reputation back if he doesn't fight you?"

Orlando shook his head, still in utter disbelief. "That's his problem," he said. "I've got my own worries. I have another mission in life. Boxing plays no part in it." He looked at Pete. "Tell them I'm not interested. Now or ever."

"It's not that simple." Pete's expression became somber. "They pulled something up out of your past, Orlando. Something you're not going to like."

"I don't like any of this," snapped Orlando, beginning to get angry now. "They can't force me to do anything. Do they think they can sue? Let them try. Remember," he said, pointing his finger at his lawyer, "that big gorilla was the one who assaulted me."

"It's got nothing to do with that," Pete explained. "They claim you're legally obligated to fight. They say they've got a contract. I don't know where they dug it up, but they faxed me a copy and I've been going over it all morning. It looks legitimate to me." He dug into his briefcase and pulled out a fax copy of the contract that Freeman had secured from Mrs. Stallings. The room was completely silent as Orlando studied it carefully for several minutes.

"This thing is ten years old," he said at last, tossing the contract back at his lawyer. "Isn't there some kind of statute of limitations on things this old?"

"Not on that one," Pete explained. "They wrote in a rider, extending the life of the contract. I think they've got you right where they want you."

"There's no piece of paper that can make my son get back into a boxing ring," Geneva wailed. "Let's just tear that thing up right here and now!"

"That won't do any good, Mrs. Leone," countered Pete. He picked up the paper and pointed out several paragraphs as he spoke. "According to this, Orlando made a deal with his trainer, Gabby Stallings, to box eight fights. Only seven of them were completed. He still owes one more fight."

Orlando nodded. "Pete's right, Mom," he said. "When I retired from the ring, I was under contract to Gabby and Alfredo. They had a fifty-fifty split, right down the middle."

"Alfredo?" asked Geneva. "Your brother owned part of your career?"

"Sure," responded Orlando. "It was for my own protection. See," he explained, "that way, they would both have to agree before any bout could be arranged. Alfredo was in for half of whatever Stallings got to look out for my interests. But when I quit, I still had one fight left to fulfill my contract." He turned to Pete. "What I don't understand is why Gabby would suddenly want to enforce a ten-year-old contract. He promised me he'd never hold me to it. He always respected my decision to leave the game. He knew what I was trying to do." Looking at Geneva, he added, "Gabby was a friend of Dad's. He always tried to help out however he could."

"Well," Pete interjected, "it's too late for Gabby to help you now."

"Get him on the phone," Orlando insisted. "I'll talk to him myself. I know he'll listen to reason."

"That's going to be difficult," Pete replied. "You see, Orlando, Gabby died a couple of years ago. He left his estate, what was left of it anyway, to his wife, Martha. And that included this old contract." He sighed and fixed his friend with a sympathetic look. "Seems like Martha sold out to the highest bidder. Walked away with a cool hundred grand."

"But," asked the bewildered Orlando, "who bought the contract?"

"Three guesses," replied Pete.

Orlando needed only one. "Sam Freeman," he said. "He's the champ's manager and mouthpiece. No one else would have the need, or the money, to do something like this."

"Bingo," replied Pete.

"Hold on just a second," demanded Geneva. "You said Gabby owned only half of the contract, isn't that right?"

"That's right," confirmed Pete, fighting the sinking feeling in the pit of his stomach. He knew exactly what was coming next.

"So that means Alfredo owns the other half," continued Geneva. "And if Alfredo is hanging on to his piece of paper, then no one can force Orlando to fight if he doesn't want to." She turned to Orlando. "Did you say they both had to agree before a match could be scheduled?"

Orlando and Geneva stared at Pete. The loophole seemed too good to be true, and both had learned from experience that when something seemed too good to be true, that usually meant it wasn't.

"Freeman's got the other half," Pete said in a voice that was barely above a whisper. "Freddie gave it to him."

Orlando's face went pale, and Geneva looked very much as if she were about to have a heart attack. "Wha . . . what?" was all she could manage to stammer.

Pete nodded, silently praying that the old expression about shooting the messenger who bears bad news wouldn't apply in this particular case. "Sam Freeman owns the whole contract, lock, stock, and barrel. If you don't honor it, he'll take you for everything you've got—besides the ministry—including the deed to the hospital, which is in your name. There's nothing I can do, Orlando. Your name is on the dotted line."

"My brother," Orlando said softly, as if speaking from a distant place in his own mind. "I can't believe he would do this to me. He's stealing my future . . . our dream . . . our vision. My own brother."

A long moment passed in complete silence as Pete and Geneva watched Orlando, waiting to see what he would do next. There was no question that, whatever was going to happen, he would be the one to make it happen. And with no room to maneuver, the choice seemed painfully obvious.

Without saying a word to either one of them, Orlando stood up, grabbed his coat off the hook on the door, and walked down the hall. Not even the kids calling out his name seemed to distract him from his resolve to reach his destination.

Freddie sat by the dazzling blue depths of his pool, while cleaners silently went about their work, scrubbing its sides with long brushes and bringing the water to the sparkling peak of inviting perfection. His country estate, not far from the mansion of Sam Freeman, had been filled with every conceivable toy and gimmick that anyone could possibly have thought to buy for a man who already had everything. Even the pool itself was the latest example of aquatic ingenuity, with a built-in Jacuzzi and a full bar where swimmers could find any drink they desired, any time of the night or day.

Basking in the warm sun, Freddie was perusing the financial pages of the daily paper. Yet as interested as he was in how his blue-chip portfolio was performing, he was having trouble concentrating on the tiny print that swam before his eyes. His mind kept going back to Orlando's wedding, to the happy faces of the guests and the simple joys they all seemed to share. *Why can't I have that kind of happiness?* he thought. *What's wrong with me and my money that people don't seem to want to hang out and get to know me?*

At that point an intercom on the patio buzzed softly. "Yes?" snapped Freddie, making no attempt to disguise his annoyance at being disturbed.

"Sir," said a voice on the other end, "your brother, a Mr. Orlando Leone, is coming out to see you. I tried to stop him, but he insisted." In the glow of the brothers' reunion, Geneva had revealed to Orlando where Freddie lived.

From across the lawn, Freddie could see Orlando heading straight for him. "I'll deal with it," he said into the intercom. He stood up, extending his hand as Orlando approached, a dark cloud of anger obscuring his face.

"Orlando," he said pleasantly, "what brings you out to my humble abode?"

Orlando knocked his brother's hand aside and stood in close, his face inches away from Freddie's. "You sold me out," he said, his voice thick with rage. "You sold out my life's work, my family, and everything I've been trying to do ever since Dad died."

"I did what I had to do," Freddie responded evenly. "Look, let's just talk about—" An open-handed slap sent him reeling backward, crashing against the lawn chairs. Angry himself now, but also with a rising fear of what his brother might do to him, Freddie scrambled to his feet, only to be slapped down again by Orlando, whose lips were compressed into a thin line as he vented his rage.

Scurrying away on his hands and knees, Freddie felt Orlando's hand on the collar of his silk shirt, dragging him to his feet. Freddie threw a desperate punch that was effortlessly blocked by his brother, who returned it with a jarring blow to the chest that knocked Freddie against the wall of the pool house. Another well-aimed punch to the torso sent him staggering back and falling onto the lawn.

For a long moment Orlando stood over his brother, his fists tightly clenched as he struggled to regain control of his emotions. Finally he loosened his grip and began shaking his head. "Look what you made me do, Alfredo," he cried out in anguish. "Look what you made me do."

Moving out from beneath Orlando's feet, Freddie stood, brushing the dirt and grass from his clothing. "If you had any sense," he snarled, "you would have bought out that contract yourself years ago."

"Why?" demanded Orlando, his voice echoing across the expanse of the lawn. "To make sure my own brother would never use it to sell me out? I never thought that day would come, Alfredo," he added bitterly.

Freddie looked around and noticed the pool cleaners standing motionless as they watched the family drama being enacted in front of them. "Get lost!" he shouted.

As they hurried away, he turned back to his brother. "Maybe you gave up on living the good life," he said with contempt. "But I didn't." With a sweep of his arm he encompassed the house and all the lush land around it. "This is all mine," he continued. "And I'm going to do anything I have to, to make sure it stays mine."

"What about the family, Alfredo?" Orlando asked, more in sorrow than anger. "What about right and wrong?"

"Don't be so naïve," Freddie responded. "You humiliated the greatest fighter in the world. You can't just walk away from something like that."

"This isn't only about Antonio Vasquez, is it?" asked Orlando.

Freddie looked at his brother for a long moment, then sighed deeply. "No," he said at last. "It's also about how you humiliated me ten years ago. Do you have any idea what it put me through to have you leave in the middle of a major boxing career? One day I'm managing the new cruiserweight champion—soon to be on his way to the heavyweight title—and the next day I'm playing nursemaid to a bunch of street punks. Have you got a clue what I had to go through to keep your nose clean after you turned your back on a whole lot of people with a whole lot of time and money invested in you?" Freddie spat out his words in anger. "I've been having to cover for you for ten years. You could be dead right now, but I've been paying the debt on the bill you owed. How do you think that makes me feel?"

"No one asked you to cover for me," Orlando reminded him.

"I'm your brother, right?" Freddie snapped back. "That's what brothers do. And now I'm trying to do something else good for you, and you come charging in here ready to take me apart with your bare hands."

"Don't give me that," Orlando countered. "This isn't about what's good for me. This is about what's good for Alfredo Leone."

"Is that right?" Freddie replied caustically. "Well, what about the million-dollar guarantee I got for you, just for showing up?"

"I don't want the money!" Orlando shouted back. "Not this way."

"Give me a break," sneered Freddie. "I've been doing a little checking up on you, brother. I know all about that run-down old hospital you sunk every last dime into. And I know that if you don't come up with the cash, like yesterday, to renovate your little dream, the city could condemn the place and you'd lose the whole thing." He looked Orlando up and down, as if taking measure of the man before him. "So don't tell me you don't want the money."

"What I need, I'll get from another source," Orlando declared calmly. "But that's probably something you'll never understand, Alfredo."

"Sure, sure," his brother said with a smirk. "I've heard all about your God and the sweet by-and-by waiting in the sky. Let me tell you something, preacher man. With twenty-to-one odds, all you've got to do is show up, dance around, and throw a few punches for a round or two. Then when the champ gets warmed up and throws something at you, just go down and stay down. You walk away with a million dollars for five minutes of work. Now that's what I call divine intervention."

Orlando stared at his brother in disbelief. "Did you say twenty-to-one odds?" he shouted. "Are you insane! I'm not a fighter! I haven't been in the ring for ten years. It's done. I'm finished."

As he started to walk away, Freddie shouted defiantly after him. "You're not just self-righteous, Orlando. You're stupid." Orlando stopped and turned around. For a moment, Freddie was afraid that his brother would come after him again. But Orlando simply stood there as if inviting Freddie to do his worst.

Taking a deep breath, he continued, "You've been a fighter all your life, Orlando. You fought in the Golden Gloves. You fought in the Olympics. And then you fought in the big leagues, where a thousand guys who weren't half as good as you dreamed they might one day get the chance that you had."

"It's over," Orlando repeated vehemently.

"Is it?" countered Freddie. "Haven't you been fighting for your precious youth center for ten years? Haven't you fought to save the bodies and souls of those street kids you collect off the corner? And aren't you fighting now to turn that hospital into a place they can call home?"

He laughed, a short, harsh bark. "Wake up, little brother," he continued. "You were born a fighter and you'll die a fighter. That's what you do. That's who you are."

Orlando crossed back over the lawn to confront his brother face-to-face. "You know something, Alfredo?" he said, locking his eyes with a steely gaze. "You're right. I am a fighter. I've always been a fighter. The only difference between then and now is that, these days, I'm fighting for something I believe in."

He jabbed his finger into Freddie's chest. "But what does that make you, big brother? You've spent your whole life running. You ran away from Mom when Dad died and she needed you the most. You ran away from your family. And mostly you ran away from God. It's time to stop running, Alfredo. It's time to stop and take a stand."

Freddie pushed his brother's hand away with contempt. "You turn this down and he'll destroy you," he said. "Sam Freeman can do that. He's got more power than you ever dreamed."

"I'm not afraid of Sam Freeman," Orlando shot back. "I know

how to take care of myself. See, big brother, I've had to learn to do things on my own. Because you were never there to protect me, like you were supposed to do. It was you who should have stepped into Dad's shoes and kept the wolves away from the door. But the funny thing is, somewhere along the line you became one of the wolves. And now I'm going to have to fight you too."

He turned on his heel and strode across the lawn, leaving Freddie slack-jawed and sputtering behind him. "You take the money, Orlando," he shouted after the retreating figure of his brother. "Don't be a fool! Just do what they want you to do. It's for your sake," he cried, before adding under his breath, "and for mine, too, little brother."

CHAPTER SIXTEEN

Orlando hammered at the punching bag, focusing all his anger and frustration on the hanging leather object, battering it mercilessly as he tried to make sense of what had happened to his life and his dreams over the past few days. Beneath the practice gloves, he could feel the constriction of the binding tape used to protect his hands and knew that, after being out of practice for so long, he was going to feel a different kind of pain in his knuckles. But far worse was the weakness he felt in his shoulders and neck as he began to work up a sweat at the punching bag. He had tried his best to stay in shape over the past ten years, but there was no denying that time had taken its toll—he was a long way from being in professional fighting condition.

Around him the noises and smells of the gym faded away as he thought back to the night before. His jabs and swings now on automatic, he recalled returning to the new apartment he and Alicia had rented, still filled with packing boxes and piled with furniture. While Darla slept peacefully on a mattress they had laid out on the floor, the newly married husband and wife tried to face together the first major crisis of their shared life.

As he poured out the story of Freddie, the contract, and the past that had come back to haunt him, Orlando watched Alicia's face go from surprise to anger to outrage and finally to warm compassion that told him, no matter what his decision might be, she would stand by him through the whole ordeal.

A sleepless night followed as he turned over again and again the options he was faced with: refuse to fight and lose everything, or agree and play into the hands of men who worshiped nothing but money and power. As dawn broke, Alicia stirred in her sleep, waking to find that Orlando wasn't next to her in bed. Rising, she looked around the apartment until she noticed an open window leading out onto the fire escape. There, Orlando knelt in prayer as the sun rose over the city, seeking the will of God for the most difficult decision of his life.

"Did you get an answer?" she asked as he came back into the apartment, and she held him tight, trying to impart some of her strength to the man she loved.

He shook his head. "Sometimes," he told her, "it seems that God isn't listening. At such times I know He wants me to trust Him. It's hard, and it would be so much easier if I got a clear signal. But that's not what this is about. He wants me to believe that, no matter what happens, He's still in control."

"So," she asked him as she kept her arms wrapped securely around him, "what are you going to do, darling?"

"I don't know," Orlando said, "I don't know." He gently disengaged from his wife and, after searching through a few boxes, found what he was looking for: the duffel bag that held his workout equipment. Then he abruptly left for the gym.

Walking through the front door of the gym, Orlando snapped out of his reverie when one of the gym trainers approached from across the room. "Phone call, Orlando," he told him and jerked his thumb in the direction of a glassed-in office in a corner of the room. "You can take it in there."

As Orlando headed for the gym office, Alicia arrived at the front door, carrying a deli take-out sack with two cups of coffee and some breakfast rolls. Unable to sleep after her husband had left for the gym, she decided that the best place for her was at his side, helping him through his agonizing decision and supporting whatever choice he finally made. After dropping off Darla at the youth center, she asked directions from a young boxer on his way to a sparring match and made her way to the main workout room. Alicia immediately spotted Orlando behind the blinds of the office window.

She could hear his angry voice, shouting into the phone. "Orlando?" she said softly as she entered the cluttered office, but all she got in return was a brief wave. The person he was talking to was getting the full brunt of his pent-up emotions.

"Listen to me," he yelled, "and listen good. Maybe you'll learn something for once in your life. The youth center has served this community faithfully for more than thirty-two years. We've been there for people, come what may. And now you're going to treat us like this—just because of some junk you hear on the news? Well, if that's the way you choose to think, go ahead. Take your children wherever you want. Better yet, why don't you take some responsibility and keep them with you." He slammed down the phone onto the receiver and turned to face his wife, his eyes still burning with rage and the veins on his forehead pulsing with his racing blood.

"Orlando," Alicia said with alarm. "Who was that?"

"The Millers," Orlando spit out.

"Orlando," she replied, crossing to him and putting a hand on his arm, "you can't talk to people that way. You're going to make the situation worse."

"Worse?" he echoed with a bitter laugh. "How could it get any worse?"

At that moment, as if in answer to his question, the sound of a scuffle could be heard outside the gym office. Moving to the door, he walked out to find two of the teenage regulars from the youth center in a knock-down-drag-out fight in the middle of the hallway. Storming over, he pulled them apart and, holding each boy at arm's length, demanded an explanation.

"We were coming down here because we heard you were going to fight the champ," one of the teens told him. "I said that I bet you could take him, and he said, 'No way.' So I let him have it."

Orlando shook both teens by the collars. "How many times do I have to tell you two to keep cool?" he said, his voice harsh and his face hardened into a stern mask. "If you keep this up, I'm going to kick you both out of the youth center for good."

The teen who had remained silent up to now erupted into a flurry of violence, striking out at Orlando. Orlando easily slipped the punch and out of pure reflex threw a short left hook to the boy's side, dropping him to the ground. A moment of shocked silence followed.

"I'm sorry," said Orlando. "I . . . didn't mean to do that."

"Yeah?" said the teen, rising to his feet. "Well, let me tell you something, Mr. Big Shot. You can't throw me out of your high-and-mighty club because I wouldn't come back, even if you got down on your knees and begged me. What everybody is saying about you is right. You're out of control." He turned to his friend. "Come on, homey," he said. "Let's let the preacher preach to himself."

Orlando turned to Alicia, a look of wordless anguish on his face. What was happening to him? What was happening to his dream? She took him by the arm. "Come on," his wife coaxed him. "Let's go home. We can sort all this out later."

"Let me get my stuff," Orlando replied, and together they returned to the workout room to retrieve his duffel bag.

The usual noises of sparring and punching bags and jumping ropes were absent as they entered. Instead, all the boxers and trainers were gathered around a television in one corner of the room. A sportscaster was talking excitedly behind a photomontage of Orlando and Vasquez, separated by a bolt of lightning.

"It's being billed as Judgment Day," the anchor was saying, looking straight into the camera. "This is payback time for the humiliating beating Antonio Vasquez received at the hands of a once unknown hotel security guard who has, virtually overnight, become one of the biggest celebrities in the sports world. Now the champ and the unknown will meet again in a fight that will undoubtedly have the whole world watching." Holding a finger to his earpiece, the anchor continued, "We're going to take you now directly to a special press conference being held by the heavyweight champion of the world."

Orlando and Alicia were about to move on when the scene switched to a crowded press conference in a hotel ballroom. Vasquez made his way to a table at the podium bristling with microphones and, taking his seat, began to address the assembled reporters.

"Mr. Orlando Leone has had the nerve to challenge me," the champ was saying, "and I have accepted. Soon I will remind the whole planet that I am still the greatest fighter in the world and no lousy hotel guard sneaking a punch when I wasn't looking is going to take that away from me."

"What's your prediction for the fight?" shouted one of the reporters from the back of the room.

"Orlando Leone is going to get hurt," said the champion as he leered into the camera. "He's going to get hurt real, real bad."

In the gym Orlando threw down his duffel bag. "That's it!" he exclaimed, drawing stares from the direction of the crowd around the television. "I never sneaked a punch on anyone in my life." He turned to Alicia. "Wait for me at home," he told her. "There's something I've got to do."

"Glad to hear that," said a voice from behind them, and Alicia and Orlando turned to see Simon standing in the doorway, dressed now in trainer's togs with a broad smile on his face.

"I just came down to see if you might need any help," he explained. "And it appears I showed up right on time."

Two hours later, Orlando, in a lather of sweat, was pounding at the punching bag once again as an assistant held it tight and Simon stood on the sidelines, urging him on. For all his determination, it was obvious that Orlando's performance was far from what it could have been: his punches were irregular and weak, and as the workout continued, each swing seemed to slow him down a little more.

"Come on, Orlando," Simon berated him. "You and I both know you ain't so out of shape that you can't even hit the bag right." He stepped forward to face the boxer. "What's wrong with you, boy? You've got to get your heart and your head into this job. Otherwise that animal is going to mop up the floor with you."

Orlando stopped punching and bent down to catch his breath. A moment later he straightened up and, slowly and deliberately, began removing the practice gloves and tape. "I can't do this," he admitted to Simon. "It's just not in me anymore." He was panting with the exertion of his workout. "It's one thing to spar to stay in shape," he continued. "But getting the killer instinct back into my soul is something I'm not ready for, Simon."

"Not ready for?" Simon echoed incredulously. "Well, you better get ready for it, son. You've got to change your whole attitude, starting right now. If you don't get yourself in the right frame of mind, Vasquez is going to cripple you." He put his hand on

Orlando's shoulder. "You and I both know that what happens here and now is going to determine what happens in that ring. You've got to be able to take at least a little punishment so you can stand up and walk out of that ring like a man when it's all over. That's what you want, isn't it?"

Orlando, whose heavy breathing had subsided, looked at the man fondly. "You know something, Simon?" he said at last. "Today is my birthday. And to tell you the truth, this isn't exactly what I wanted to find myself doing when I turned forty."

"Forty?" Simon repeated, letting out a loud hoot. "You're forty?" As Orlando nodded, he laughed again and slapped him on the back. "Shoot, boy," he declared. "Don't you know life just begins at forty? I'd be out there in that ring myself if today was my fortieth birthday. Now, come on! Show me what you've got."

Orlando couldn't help laughing at Simon's stern admonition, and after redonning the tape and practice gloves, he returned to the punching bag with renewed vigor. Maybe forty wasn't so old, after all.

By the time the day's regimen of relentless exercise and hard and fast sparring was over, however, Orlando felt as if he were eighty instead of forty. As he hauled his aching carcass up the stairway to the new apartment, he could think only of a hot shower and a warm bed. *Scratch the shower,* he thought. *I'm going to take a direct dive between the sheets.*

The apartment was dark as he entered, and from the silence he assumed that Alicia and Darla must still be out shopping for the household necessities that every new home requires. He moved wearily into the living room, and by the streetlight shining through the window, he noticed that Alicia had worked hard to put furniture and personal belongings in their proper places. *It is beginning to be comfortable,* Orlando thought, relishing the prospect of climbing into bed and wondering if he had the energy to actually take off his clothes before he fell asleep.

At that moment, the lights went on, and in the sudden glare, Alicia and Darla popped out from behind the sofa. The little girl held a birthday cake in her hands, brightly lit with forty candles.

"Happy birthday!" they shouted in unison and rushed up to welcome him home with hugs and kisses. Setting the cake down on the kitchen table, they watched as he blew out the candles, not knowing the effort it required even to take a deep breath.

"Can I have a piece of cake?" Darla asked as she picked the smoking candles out of the icing.

"We'll all have one," Alicia replied while taking plates and forks from the cupboard.

"Not for me," said Orlando. "It looks good, but I've got to stick to a regimen if I'm going to get ready for Vasquez."

"But it's your birthday cake," said a disappointed Darla. "We made it ourselves . . . from scratch."

"Come on, honey," Alicia joined in. "Just a little piece. How can that hurt?"

"I said no," Orlando replied sharply, "and I meant no." He got up from the table and, crossing the room, entered the bedroom and slammed the door behind him.

Darla gave her mother a heartbroken look. "Doesn't he like our cake?" she asked.

On the other side of the bedroom door, Orlando collapsed, fully clothed, onto the bed, but instead of passing immediately into the deep sleep he craved, he lay with his eyes wide open and his mind in turmoil as he replayed the events of the day and tried again to find a way around the dilemma he was in through no fault of his own.

After a few minutes he heard a soft knock on the door, and

Alicia stuck her head in. "Honey?" she said softly. "Mind if I come in for a moment?"

Orlando sat up and swung his legs over the side of the bed, putting his head in his hands. "I'm sorry, Alicia," he said. "I know you two worked hard. It's just been a very long day."

"Tell me about it," Alicia replied, sitting next to him and stroking his head. "That's what I'm here for."

He turned to her. "I really don't know if I can do this, Alicia," he confessed. "Even that birthday cake you two made. I'm sure it's delicious. And if I had one bite, I'd probably go on and eat a whole lot more than I should."

"I don't understand," Alicia responded. "You don't have a weight problem. You're in better shape than most men half your age."

"I'm in training," Orlando told her. "It's like putting yourself through the most extreme discipline there is. If I ate that cake, it might trigger a whole bunch of other food cravings—cheese, fries, hamburgers—and the next thing you know I'd be waddling into the ring gasping for breath. This is a whole new way of life . . . a way of life you know nothing about."

Darla came into the bedroom, rubbing her eyes. "I'm tired, Mommy," she whined.

"Go ahead," said Orlando, taking Alicia's hand and squeezing it. "You take care of her. I'll be fine."

The look on Alicia's face reflected her doubts about his comforting words, but she stood up and led Alicia away. Orlando lay back down on the bed with a groan. Before his head hit the pillow, he had fallen fast asleep.

The light of a new morning was just beginning to break from outside the window when he woke again to find his head cradled in Alicia's lap as she stroked his hair gently. Still groggy, he turned his head to look up at her smiling face. "How long was I out?" he asked.

"All night," she replied. "I made sure nothing would disturb you." He reached up and pulled her down to him for a lingering kiss, and when it was over, she stretched out beside him and whispered in his ear. "What's happening to you, darling?" she asked.

Orlando answered without looking at her. "What do you want me to say?" he replied. "I'm between a rock and a hard place, and I've got no way out."

"It's just that," she began hesitantly, "you haven't been yourself ever since this whole boxing match came up."

"I know," he answered, staring up at the dim light on the ceiling. "I can feel it myself. There's a part of me that I wanted to be dead and gone. But now it's starting to come back."

"What part?" she asked.

"The fighting part." His tone was terse. "The part that says it's better to lash out before someone does it to you first. The part that believes the only way to make it in this world is to be the toughest, meanest customer on the block. The part that feels safe only when it's in control."

"You're safe with me," she whispered and held him tight.

"Maybe we're safe here," he replied. "Just the three of us. But in the ring it's different. There, all you've got to depend on is the skills you've developed through the sweat and blood of youth." He turned to her for the first time. "And I honestly don't have those skills anymore."

"Of course you do," she insisted, leaning on one elbow. "I've heard everyone say you were one of the best. That's not something you lose. Once you know how it's done, all you've got to do is get back into practice again."

"It's not that easy," Orlando told her as the first sounds of the stirring city could be heard in barking dogs and delivery trucks starting their rounds. "I may still have the technique, but there are unavoidable physical limitations that come with age."

"But you're still a young man!" she interjected.

"Not for the boxing game. When you get into your thirties, your time is limited. The first things to go are the legs. You just can't dance away from danger like you used to." Orlando looked her straight in the eye. "Have you ever had one of those dreams where you're being chased by a monster and you can't seem to get your legs moving fast enough—like you're running through water?" She nodded, her eyes wide. "That's what it's like," he explained. "Then you start to lose your speed, your hand-eye coordination. You see an opening to throw a punch. You let one go, only it never connects. You're punching at air because your target has had that split second to move somewhere else."

He disengaged from her and sat on the edge of the bed, his back to Alicia. "It works the other way around too," he continued without looking at her. "Say Vasquez throws a punch. I see it coming, I know what to do to get out of the way, but I can't make my body move fast enough to avoid getting nailed. And that's what's going to happen, round after round, until I'm a piece of human hamburger."

"I can't believe that," replied Alicia, sitting next to him and putting her small hands around his well-developed biceps. "Look at you," she continued. "You're so strong. You keep yourself in great shape. And you've got months to prepare for this bout."

"It's not about strength," replied Orlando with sudden intensity, and he turned to face her again. "Strength is nothing without good reflexes and timing. That night at the hotel—Vasquez could have handed me my teeth if his reflexes hadn't been slowed down by alcohol. Plus he was in the hotel, which is my turf. When we're in the ring, it's going to be his world, and you can believe he'll be stone-cold sober. I can't use any fancy jujitsu or full frontal tackles or police handcuffs when I'm in there."

His eyes were bright and burning now, and their intensity was almost frightening to Alicia. "The truth is, I don't know if I've got what it takes to make this even competitive." He buried his head in his hands. "Forget that," he continued after a moment. "I don't know if I've got what it takes to finish."

CHAPTER SEVENTEEN

REGARDLESS OF THE DOUBTS AND INNER TORMENT HE FELT, Orlando was back at the gym within a few hours of his early morning conversation with Alicia, trying to work out some of the stiffness and pain in his joints and muscles with a series of stretching exercises. As he concentrated on his routine, Pete and Simon entered the exercise room escorting a beefy young man who Orlando could immediately tell was no stranger to the ring.

"Orlando," said Pete, "I'd like you to meet Mike Konshak." As the two boxers shook hands, the lawyer explained, "Mike is currently ranked number six in the world, and he's got a style very similar to the champ's."

Orlando nodded. "I've seen your work," he told the fighter. "I'd say you're going places."

"That means a lot coming from you, Mr. Leone," Konshak replied.

"Mike has agreed to go a few rounds with you, Orlando," Simon interjected, "just to give us an idea of how much progress you've been making and what we still need to work on."

"I appreciate it," Orlando told the young fighter.

"It's my pleasure," Konshak said with a smile as the two moved toward a sparring ring where two trainers were on hand to prep them for the match. By the time the bell rang on the first of the practice rounds, a small group of curious onlookers had gathered, including several veterans of the gym and the young Olympic boxer Erik West, who had expressed such admiration for Orlando a few short weeks ago.

The expression on West's face mirrored the attitude of most of the onlookers. Their skepticism was evident as Orlando closed in for the attack, his movements jumpy and his jabs nervous and falling short of the mark. They knew only too well exactly what Orlando had been trying to tell his wife earlier that day: he was out of his league, not just squaring off against the champ, but even against the brash young fighter in the ring with him now. Orlando Leone Jr., in short, had seen his best days.

As Simon stood in Orlando's corner, muttering encouragement and wincing every time one of Konshak's jarring blows found its mark, Pete sat on the nearby bleachers, trying to resist the temptation to cover his eyes from the painful sight of his friend being completely outmatched. A quick combination sent Orlando reeling for the ropes, and for a moment it seemed that he was about to drop to his knees. Then drawing on some reserve of strength that surprised those watching, he moved back into the ring and expertly set up his opponent for one of his trademark overhand rights. For once the punch connected, and Konshak seemed momentarily stunned by its impact. But he quickly shook off its effects and launched a furious attack that had Orlando back into the ropes as the bell rang.

Two rounds later, dripping with sweat and groaning with each blow that found its mark, Orlando at last heard the bell ring. The sparring match was over, and it was all he could do to shake hands with Konshak and shamble back to his corner. The last thing he saw before heading to the showers was the disappointed look on Erik West's face as the young fighter turned his back on his onetime hero.

The morning's workout over, Orlando packed his duffel bag and headed back to the youth center. The day had broken clear and bright, with a snap to the air, but Orlando hardly noticed what was happening around him. Deeply depressed and lost in his own hopeless thoughts, he avoided the small groups of teenagers playing hoops in the front yard of the center and headed straight for his office, where he slowly lowered himself into his desk chair and sat in the gloomy half light that leaked through the blinds.

That was when he heard the tentative notes of a child's hands picking out a melody on piano keys, a melody that brought with it memories of another, simpler time. Rising slowly from his chair, he followed the sound down the hall to the youth center's music room where he found Darla sitting at the piano bench with her mother at her side.

"Hey, ladies," he greeted them with a smile. Even in the midst of his troubles, it was good to see these familiar and loving faces.

The delighted Darla jumped up and ran to hug him, wrapping her small arms around his knees. "Will you play the song for me, Daddy?" she asked, looking up at his face, her large brown eyes bright with joy.

"What song?" was Alicia's curious question from the piano bench.

"It's nothing, really," replied Orlando modestly. "Just a little song I sang for Darla a while back. It's kind of our song."

"Well, what do you know?" said Alicia, crossing her arms. "I learn something new about you every day. I had no idea that you were a boxer who did floor shows."

"And I'm not much good at either one of them," responded the chagrined Orlando.

"We'll be the judges of that," Alicia replied. "Won't we, Darla?"

The child nodded gravely as Orlando took his place at the piano and began to play a soft and gentle melody with surprising fluidness and grace. The song had a sweet yet hauntingly old-fashioned air to it, like something from the turn of the century. Alicia's eyes filled with tears as her daughter watched Orlando's every subtle move.

"I'll always love you," he sang with a clear and unwavering voice. "I'll always care. You are the one love to whom none compare. When skies are gray and friends are untrue, I'll be that someone who'll watch over you." Orlando's voice was deep but unusually sensitive. "When life is over, when all is said and done, you will have always been my number one." Orlando looked straight into Darla's eyes and sang, "Always remember wherever you are, I'll always love you, sweetheart."

The last note faded to the sound of Alicia's applause. "That was beautiful," she said as she dried her eyes. "How come I never heard it before?"

Orlando smiled. "It was our little secret," he confided. "You see, Darla and I have always had a thing for each other." He ruffled the child's hair as she looked up at him with a broad smile.

"I'm glad you're my daddy," the little girl said. "I prayed every night that it would be you."

"So that's how it happened," Orlando said with a laugh, and he picked up Darla and held her in his arms. "Well, I'm sure glad I was the one who got the job."

"Daddy," she continued, looking straight into his eyes, "when you win the fight with the other man, will everyone know that it was Jesus who helped you?"

Now it was Orlando's turn to fight back a flood of tears. "I'm sorry, Darla," he said, choking back his emotion. "But the only thing people are going to learn about Jesus is what He looked like when He got crucified."

"Orlando," Alicia said in a low voice, "please don't say that." She smiled brightly as she took Darla from his arms. "What Daddy means," she told the child, "is that Jesus will be helping Daddy, no matter what happens."

"But isn't he going to win?" her daughter asked fearfully.

"Darla," Orlando interjected, "I want you to listen to me very carefully. I can't make any promises about winning this fight. But I can promise that, no matter what happens, Daddy will always love you."

Alicia looked straight at him. "You're going to win. Don't you always win?"

Orlando shook his head sadly. "I wish I could believe that," he replied as Alicia set Darla down on the piano bench and the child began to softly pick out the notes of the song he had sung. "But I'm not fighting for the right reason. To tell you the truth, I'm only in this situation because my past has come back to haunt me. I should never have put on a boxing glove in my life. Maybe that's why I just can't put my heart into this thing. Because I never had the feeling that God was backing me on this."

"Of course He is—" Alicia began before Orlando silenced her by putting his finger to her lips.

"Please," he begged her. "Just hear me out." He took a deep breath. "I'm in this fight because of a wrong choice I made a long time ago. The choice to impress my brother instead of seeking God's will for my life."

His voice quavered as he forced out the bitter memories. "I should never have gotten involved in boxing in the first place. That wasn't my calling. It never was." His arm swept around the room to encompass the entire youth center. "This was my calling.

It's my life mission to raise the money, do the work, fight whatever wars I have to fight to see this center up and alive. It's my purpose in life. I wasn't ever supposed to win championships. I was supposed to win souls." Tears coursed down his cheeks as the next words formed on his lips. "I learned that too late. And now I've got to pay for that mistake."

Both Orlando and Alicia noticed that Darla had stopped playing. They looked down at the child, who climbed up onto the piano bench to dry the tears as they fell down Orlando's face. "Don't worry, Daddy," she told him. "I believe God's betting on you to win, and the devil's betting on you to lose. So I guess your vote decides the election."

Orlando looked from his daughter to his wife and back again as a slow revelation dawned on his face. "Maybe you're right," he said at last, with excitement growing in his voice. "Maybe I've missed something so simple all along."

He turned to Alicia and, hugging her, covered her face with kisses, then gave Darla the same loving treatment. "You have given me an idea," he told Darla as he started to cross to the door of the music room.

"Where are you going?" asked Alicia, alarmed at his sudden and erratic behavior.

"I'll explain later," he cried over his shoulder. "Just give me two days."

"Two days?" echoed the stunned Alicia. "But why?"

"I've got to ask for a couple of favors," he replied as he disappeared down the hallway.

Darla and Alicia looked at each other. "A couple of favors?" they replied at the same time.

It was bright and sunny the next morning as Orlando made his way across the rich green lawn and onto the path that led around a spacious house to a shimmering blue swimming pool. Even before he reached the chair where his brother sat under an umbrella, Alfredo had seen him coming and stood up, uncertain why he was being paid this visit.

Orlando wasted no time. "I have a favor to ask," he said as a bird began to sing in the tress at the lawn's edge. Anyone who might have been watching from that vantage point would have seen the two brothers engage in deep conversation, a conversation that ended with a sudden and heartfelt embrace. Whatever was said between these men, it was obvious that a reconciliation had begun to take place. Then, as suddenly as he arrived, Orlando left, walking back down the path as his brother watched.

Later that day, a rental car pulled up the long driveway that led to a beautiful and stately old country house on the wide, meandering banks of a river. The late afternoon light cast golden shadows through the trees, their leaves the deep russet tones of autumn. The car pulled to a stop at the front door of the estate, and a moment later Orlando emerged. Taking a moment to breathe the cool, crisp air, he walked briskly to the front door and rang the bell.

When the door opened, a face familiar both to him and to millions of fighting fans around the world beamed happily in greeting.

"Orlando Leone," said the internationally renowned boxer Sugar Ray Leonard. "How long has it been, man?"

"Not since the Olympics, Sugar Ray," Orlando replied as the two former teammates embraced. "And there's been a lot of water under the bridge since then."

"You've got that right," said Sugar Ray, making way for his friend and leading him into a spacious den decorated with souvenirs from his illustrious career. Sitting down on the sofa, his host offered Orlando a soft drink before asking him the inevitable question. "So," said Sugar Ray, leaning back into the plush cushions, "what brings you back into my life after all these years?"

"It's a long but obvious story, Ray," Orlando replied.

"I've got all night if that's what it takes," answered the famous boxer as he settled back to hear a story that, even as Orlando told it, he could hardly believe had actually happened to him.

"Man, that's one for the books," said Sugar Ray after Orlando had brought him up to date. "And you say Freddie was behind all this?"

"My brother and I have come to an agreement," revealed Orlando to his old friend. "He was the first person I met with on my little two-day jaunt. It's funny . . . even though he didn't have any qualms about double-crossing me, when it came time to make things right, it was almost as if he'd been waiting for the chance. I guess they know what they're talking about when they say that family ties are the strongest of them all. Even greed and fear can't break them."

"So Freddie's going to help you?" queried Sugar Ray, intrigued by this new turn of events. "But how?"

Orlando leaned forward. "Sugar," he said, "I've got to keep that to myself for right now. What's important is that I get into shape and find a strategy to fight the champ. And for that I need your help." He reached out and grasped the boxer's arm. "This is my Marvin Hagler, and you're the only one who can put together the kind of world-class game plan I need to pull it off. Will you do it for me, friend, for old times' sake?"

"Forget old times," Sugar Ray replied with a smile. "I'll do it for tomorrow's sake. For your tomorrow . . . and that newfound family of yours." He stood up. "But we better get started right away. We've got to really think through this one. You're lucky I've been following this guy Vasquez's career for a while now. I've got his moves down cold, and I know exactly where his weak points are."

"Just like you did with Tommy Hearns?" Orlando asked.

"Even more so. Vasquez is bigger than Tommy, but he's more predictable. I know how to frustrate this guy. If I was two hundred pounds, I'd go do it myself." They laughed.

"I knew I could depend on you," Orlando told him, and the love that passed between the two men was as strong in its way as any family bond.

It was deep in the middle of the night when Simon was awakened from a sound sleep. Rising slowly from his bed and tying his threadbare old robe around his waist, he shuffled to the front door and put his eye up to the peephole.

"Lord," he said under his breath at the sight that greeted him on the other side. "What are you up to now?" Opening the locks, he stepped aside while Orlando and Sugar Ray burst in.

"Sugar Ray Leonard!" Simon exclaimed in utter amazement before turning to Orlando. "You're about to give me a heart attack, son. What's going on?"

"No time for that now," Orlando replied. "We've got a lot of work to do."

"What sort of work?" asked the bewildered pastor.

Sugar Ray laughed and slapped Orlando on the back. "We've got to help this old man steal someone's thunder," he replied. "Steal it fair and square."

"I'm hearing what you're saying," Simon responded in amazement. "But I'm not at all sure that I believe it." He turned to Orlando and asked, "Aren't you the same Orlando Leone who was telling everyone how you couldn't face down the champ one-on-one in a fair fight?"

"Something's changed, Simon," replied the excited Orlando. "Don't ask me what. Just trust me. I'm ready to go to war."

Simon let out a little whoop. "That's the best news I've heard all month!" he shouted. "We've got ourselves a warrior ready to go to war."

"Not quite ready," Orlando reminded him. "There's still a lot of work to be done between now and the main event. I've got to get myself in the best shape of my life. I've got to bring back everything I once knew about this game. I've got to study my opponent and get to know his moves better than I know my own." He put his arms around the preacher and the puncher. "That's where you two guys come in."

"Well, what are we waiting for?" exclaimed Sugar Ray. "Let's build us a champion!"

CHAPTER EIGHTEEN

THE SEARCHLIGHT PROBED THE DARK NIGHT SKY AS, HIGH above, blimps and helicopters hovered, recording the awesome scene. The streets had been shut down for blocks in every direction in a radius around the sports arena, but that didn't stop the crowds from gathering to witness the media-hyped moment, even if it was at a distance. Long limos, black, white, and silver, honked their horns as they inched forward through the mob, crawling toward the police checkpoints that would allow them access to the restricted area and the special parking sections that had been set aside for the VIPs from every corner of the world.

Inside the perimeter, souvenir hawkers peddled T-shirts and baseball caps, programs and coffee mugs—anything and everything that bore the now universally familiar logo that showed the faces of Antonio Vasquez and Orlando Leone Jr. separated by a jagged bolt of lightning. Men in tuxes smoking long cigars escorted women in evening gowns and glittering jewels through the throng, holding up their tickets at the gates as if they were allowed entrance to heaven itself. Scalpers were nowhere to be seen: every seat in the massive arena had been sold out for weeks, for amounts of money that a family in a developing nation could live on for a year.

Inside the high-domed arena, the excitement was reaching a hysterical pitch as fight time neared. In spite of the mandatory, mediocre undercard match that was included on the program, everyone was really there to see one thing and one thing only— the grudge battle between the heavyweight champion of the world, Antonio Vasquez, and the most unlikely underdog in the history of boxing, Orlando Leone Jr.

High above the ring, glowing a dazzling white beneath the spotlight trained on them, were two huge banners hung from the rafters. The faces of Vasquez and Leone squared off in the vast expanse of the sports center, more like gods than mortal men, ready to do combat from the very heights of Mount Olympus while mere mortals stood by and watched in awe.

For the millions upon millions of pay-per-view customers, the thrill and energy of the event were being pumped live and direct into their television sets. Two sports announcers in bright blue blazers provided commentary from high above in a skybox reserved for the press. All around them, the world media were in a frenzy of anticipation. Tonight was the night.

"We're coming to you live and direct," said the older announcer, his silver hair gleaming in the bright lights. "And if I can dare say it, this has to be the most unusually electrifying event in the entire history of the sport of boxing."

"No truer words were ever spoken, Jim," enthused the second announcer, a younger man with slicked-back hair. "I've been in the sports broadcast business for a long time, and I can't ever remember having seen this much excitement and anticipation for a match."

"Of course," interjected the first commentator, "this is no ordinary match, is it? After all, we're looking at the reigning heavyweight champion of the world going toe to toe with a newcomer." He chuckled. "Except in this case there's not much that's actually 'new' about Orlando Leone Jr. This former cruiserweight champion recently turned forty years old, almost twice the age of the champ."

"Which might explain the odds we're looking at tonight," added the younger anchor. "Buster Douglas wasn't even expected to be competitive when he defeated Mike Tyson, but how often do you see that kind of miracle in this game?"

As the media continued to examine the evening's coming contest from every conceivable angle, the attendees began to find their seats, and the clock ticked steadily down to fight time, Orlando sat in his locker room, deeply engaged in a last-minute conference with Simon and Sugar Ray. "Come in," he said as a knock sounded at the door.

A security guard entered. "Sorry to disturb you," he said, "but there's a lady here who keeps trying to tell me she's your wife, Mr. Leone. I said no one was allowed back here but—" Alicia suddenly appeared in the doorway behind the guard and pushed her way through. "Hey!" he shouted, but Orlando waved him aside.

"I wouldn't get in that one's way," he said with a chuckle. "She looks like one tough customer."

"I had to see you before this all began," Alicia said, the emotion in her voice clear for anyone to hear. Simon and Sugar Ray exchanged a quick look.

"We've, uh, got some details to talk over," the pastor said. "Ray and I will be out in the hall."

As the guard followed them out of the locker room, Alicia turned to her husband. "Orlando," she said, trying hard to fight back tears, "I just want you to know . . ."

"It's okay," he said, reaching out with his taped hands and holding her close. "You don't have to say it. I can see it in your eyes."

"I love you," she whispered and kissed him passionately to prove the commitment of her words.

After a long moment their lips parted and Orlando smiled. "You head on down and take your seat now," he told her. "I'll see you when this is over." He reached out and stroked her cheek. "And don't worry. I've been down this road before. It's in God's hands now."

Alicia could not stop the tears from flowing as she gazed deeply at her husband's handsome, rugged face. She wondered whether she would ever see it in this condition again and tossed a silent prayer to the God she had only just been introduced to, for the protection of this very special man. With a reassuring nod, Orlando sent her on her way. The time had come. The test was at hand. He folded his hands, the tape still sticky on his flesh, and began a silent prayer.

Across the hall, in the locker room of Antonio Vasquez, a far different scene was being played out. A half dozen trainers were prepping the champ for the fight, rubbing him down and psyching him up. The head trainer leaned over him as the thick gloves were being laced up and whispered hoarsely in his ear. "It's time, Champ," he intoned. "It's time to go out there and take back what belongs to you. Show this fool who he messed with! Prove to the whole world how easily you can squash him like a bug! It's payback time, Champ! This is where he gets what's coming to him."

Outside in the lobby, two very different groups of people were arriving as well. From one entrance, Sam Freeman with Freddie and an entourage of garish women and men in shiny suits and sunglasses came down the aisle like a royal procession and took their seats at ringside. From the opposite entrance, Geneva and a gaggle of teenagers from the youth center took their seats near Orlando's corner. Pete, who had been at ringside since the doors opened, nodded and waved nervously at them. He looked at his watch: five minutes until fight time.

Sugar Ray and Simon had returned to Orlando's locker room not just to convey last-minute advice and counsel but also to impart a blessing for protection and favor from God. With them were several older men, friends of Simon who made up his weekly prayer circle. Simon laid his hands on top of the fighter's head.

"Lord," he said in a gentle but clear voice, "I ask You tonight that the same spirit that came upon Samson to give him strength to fight the Philistines, the same spirit that gave David the courage to face Goliath, will fall upon our brother Orlando tonight." A gentle round of "amens" echoed in agreement.

At ringside, near where Geneva and the youth center contingent had settled, Alicia found her seat next to Darla.

"Ladies and gentlemen!" the announcer boomed as Darla, frightened by the sounds, clutched at her mother's hand. "Welcome to tonight's main event. A title fight for the heavyweight championship of the world!"

The crowd erupted into a roar, loud rock music blared from the PA system, and the house lights dimmed. A brilliant spot illuminated Orlando where he stood at the top of a ramp of stairs leading back into the rear of the hall. As he made his way to the ring, wearing a robe of bright Olympic blues, a mix of cheers and boos greeted him. Ringing out above the roar of the crowd was the pounding dance remix version of the old hymn and Olympic theme "Joyful, Joyful, We Adore Thee." The kids from the youth center sang along at the top of their lungs.

"And here comes the contender!" exclaimed the younger commentator, barely able to suppress his excitement as Orlando reached the ring and climbed up to his corner. "Orlando Leone Jr., the hotel security guard who shocked the world a few months back by taking out the reigning heavyweight champion in a penthouse brawl. Hardly a stranger to the ring, Leone was a former cruiserweight champion who fought undefeated from 1985 to 1988."

"And from up here, it looks like Leone has gotten himself back into fighting trim," commented the silver-haired newsman. "Of course, it's anyone's guess if Leone might be able to display anything that resembles championship material, but if Antonio Vasquez is expecting a pushover tonight, I think he might be in for something of a surprise."

A pounding Latin beat announced the arrival of the champ from the other side of the building. The blinding spotlight glanced off his fiery red robe as he danced and pranced down the aisle toward the ring.

"That music can mean only one thing," the older anchor continued. "Antonio Vasquez is in the house. And I've got to say that the world champion for three consecutive years looks like he's very much ready to take care of a little business here tonight."

From his ringside seat, Freeman rose to his feet and clapped in time to the music. Freddie stood as well, but to anyone who might have been watching closely, the nervous flicker of his eyes and the hesitant clap of his hands revealed his divided loyalties.

Climbing into the ring, Vasquez fixed Orlando with a steely glare that hardly seemed interrupted by a blink.

"With that red robe," the younger announcer was saying, "Vasquez looks like nothing so much as a supremely confident matador getting ready to show the little bull who's boss."

"Well, one thing's for sure," added his partner, "the champ has plenty of reason to want vengeance here tonight. The events at that downtown hotel, which people are calling an 'unofficial upset,' left him with a lot to undo in the eyes of the public. And tonight he seems determined to redeem himself."

From her seat near Orlando's corner, Alicia watched, her hand covering her mouth, with a growing sense of misgiving as the two fighters took their places diagonally across the ring from each other. Once again the announcer's voice echoed across the standing-room-only crowd.

"In the blue corner," came the booming call, "weighing in at one hundred and ninety pounds, the former WBA cruiserweight champion and Olympic Bronze medallist with a record of twenty-eight wins with nineteen knockouts and no defeats, from Brooklyn, New York . . . Orlando Leone Jr."

The applause that greeted his name was mostly centered around the crowd from the youth center, who launched into a noisy demonstration of support. Orlando stood with his head bowed, seemingly oblivious to the introductions or even the supporting pat on the back he received from Simon.

"And in the red corner," the announcer continued, "weighing in at two hundred and thirty-five pounds of pure destructive power, from Las Vegas, Nevada, with a record of thirty-seven wins with thirty-seven knockouts, the undefeated, undisputed heavyweight champion of the world, Antonio 'the Body Snatcher' Vasquez!"

Acknowledging the deafening roar, Vasquez lifted his gloved hands high over his head and bobbed up and down in his corner. His trainer removed his silk robe as Simon did the same for Orlando, and both fighters continued to loosen up their muscles with short, dancing steps.

"I'm afraid, Mommy," said Darla, clutching Alicia's hand from the seat next to her.

"I know, honey," replied her mother without taking her eyes off Orlando. "I am too."

The referee entered the ropes and called both fighters to the center of the ring. "You both know the rules," he told them. "Let's have a good clean fight." He paused, looking at them. "Let's rock and roll." Antonio and Orlando briefly knocked gloves before returning to their respective corners.

As Simon gave the fighter a last-minute rubdown, another trainer from the gym squirted water into his open mouth and then fitted his mouthpiece across his teeth. From his seat directly below Orlando's corner, Sugar Ray climbed up on the ropes and whispered into the ear of his former Olympic teammate.

"He's just a man, Orlando," he told him. "Remember that. Only flesh and blood, just like you. He can be beaten. Don't let the macho image and all that big talk get in the way. Duran tried that with me, and I still beat him. You can do the same. He's gonna come stormin' at you real strong, so keep your concentration. Pick your shots and you'll be fine."

But the moment for advice, encouragement, or second thoughts was over. To the clanging echo of the bell and the deafening roar of the crowd, the fight was on.

True to form, Vasquez immediately moved in tight on Orlando, letting loose with a flurry of punches. Whatever apprehensions he might have had about the ordeal he was about to endure, the first barrage of blows cemented them in Orlando's mind. He was in for a long and brutal evening. Shaking his head to clear his mind, he brought his full attention to the game plan he had so painstakingly worked out with Sugar Ray during the previous weeks. Sticking and moving, jabbing and evading, staying out of a macho punching match, Orlando focused totally on scoring points and keeping himself alive and evasive.

"The champ has wasted no time in giving Leone a taste of what's in store," related the older commentator into the microphone. "It seemed for a moment there that Leone was taken completely off guard, but now a little less than two minutes into the first round, the challenger seems to have regained his balance and is giving the champ a run for his money."

"This looks to me like a textbook example of classic boxing technique," observed his partner. "Leone obviously knows this game inside and out. But how long can those forty-year-old legs keep this up?"

In the blinding light of the ring, Orlando saw the champ telegraphing a right hook and quickly slipped under it. But before he could retaliate, a surprise left connected with his midsection, and he could feel the wind knocked out of his lungs. Dancing back, he bought himself a few seconds out of Vasquez's range to regain his bearings. As if from a great distance, he heard Sugar Ray shouting from the corner, "Get your legs back under you. Keep him off balance! Don't let him get into his rhythm!"

From her ringside seat, Alicia's initial rush of horror at seeing the punishment her husband was enduring quickly turned to a warm glow of pride as she saw him bring his skills and abilities into play. It was obvious that he was calling on innate fighting instincts that had been hidden away for a decade.

"Your daddy knows what he's doing," she shouted to Darla above the roar of the crowd. "This is a side of him I've never seen before," she added, more to herself than to her daughter.

But regardless of his training, regardless of the long hours he had put into preparing for this night, the punishment being doled out by Vasquez was taking its toll. "Leone is putting up valiant resistance," shouted the younger announcer, "but he's really taking a beating to the body in there."

"Keep moving, and stay off the ropes," Sugar Ray shouted from across the vast distance of the canvas.

The champ moved in closer again, and Orlando could clearly see another roundhouse right on its way. Ducking it like a man getting out of the way of an oncoming 747, Orlando arched back quickly and delivered a jarring left hook to the champ's jaw. The effect was immediate. Vasquez staggered, took two steps back and, for one dazed moment, didn't seem to know where he was. The sound of the cheering crowd rattled Orlando's eardrums as the older announcer shouted, "It looks like Leone has gotten in his first good shot of the match, a beautifully timed left hook."

Pulling himself together, the champ, with a look of pure bloodlust in his eyes, charged Orlando. Dodging the assault a second time, Orlando landed two more strong hooks just above Vasquez's rib cage. In the next second the fighters were locked, and as the referee tried to pull them apart, the bell announcing the end of the first round clanged. For a moment it seemed as if neither fighter knew the round was over. Standing chest to chest and nose to nose, they glared at each other, as if the screaming crowd didn't even exist. There was no longer any doubt in the mind of anyone watching—this was personal.

While the fighters returned to their corners, it was time for the sports commentators to sum up the action at the end of the first round. "Three minutes into this unexpectedly competitive fight," remarked the younger of the two, "and it looks like Leone, after taking a real beating in the early moments of Round One, has gotten into his stride. But by the time the bell rang, there seemed to be some very bad blood between these two determined fighters."

"You can say that again," remarked his partner. "In his first heavyweight fight of any kind, Leone has already proven to Vasquez that he won't be taken for granted. If I had to guess, I'd say Leone clearly won this round on points. We'll see what the judges say, but from here, it looks like we can chalk one up for the challenger."

While the crowd seethed around them, Orlando and Vasquez were getting separate pep talks as trainers sprayed water on their faces and rubbed down their arm muscles.

"You've got him scared," an exultant Sugar Ray told his friend. "He may not be showing it, but even from here I can smell the fear on him. He thought this was going to be easy, but you're proving him wrong. You're proving them all wrong."

"Show him who's boss, Champ," Vasquez's trainer urged his fighter. "The only reason he's still out there is that he's too dumb to know when he's overmatched. You've got to teach him a lesson he'll never forget. Punish him! Punish him!"

"Watch the distance," Sugar Ray counseled. "This guy is a power hitter. Don't forget that. Whatever you do, don't let him get a full extension on that right. Remember, Orlando! You've got nothing to prove. Just keep jabbing and stay out of the way. And keep moving to his left. Don't let him get set."

The bell announcing the second round echoed through the arena. Orlando moved into the ring aggressively, knowing there was no turning back now. *God, help me,* he prayed silently as he raised his fists to engage his enemy. Orlando's wartime mentality was coming back more quickly than he thought.

CHAPTER NINETEEN

FOR THE NEXT SEVERAL ROUNDS, ORLANDO STUCK CLOSE to the game plan Sugar Ray had devised: jab, jab, jab, move left, avoid the right-hand power shots, stay off the ropes, and rack up the points. It was a costly strategy, in terms of his stamina. But it appeared that if he could keep up this pace, he would have a clean, decisive win. If it came to winning on points, it was anyone's guess who would emerge the champ. By the time Orlando flopped down on his stool after Round Five, he knew that his reserves of strength were rapidly being depleted.

Returning to his corner, he waited for the trainer to remove his mouthpiece before telling Sugar Ray his assessment. "Ray," he said between deep, ragged breaths, "if I don't put this gorilla away in the next round, I don't know how much more of this I can take. I've got to stop him now, or I won't be able to run for six more rounds."

"You find that opening and go for it, all the way," Sugar Ray urged. "This guy's a sucker for an overhand right, especially after he finishes his third jab. What you've got to do is wait till after his third jab snaps out there. He'll drop it, then you come over the top with the biggest haymaker you can find. Then double up on it. He'll be hurt. Trust me. He's ready."

The bell rang, and with a deep, inward groan, Orlando returned to the battle.

Sugar Ray's encouraging words seemed to give Orlando a new determination as he stepped into the ring for the sixth round. He unleashed a furious attack, pouring out all his strength, all his rage, and all his determination, as if the champion were the sole cause of everything that stood in the way of his hopes and dreams. He had to bring down Vasquez in this round. It was his only chance for survival, and he held nothing back.

It was then, with thirty seconds left before the bell, that he saw his chance to accomplish the impossible . . . his only chance for survival. As the crowd screamed itself hoarse, Orlando came in tight and fast with an expertly timed series of blows that threw Vasquez completely off balance. Vasquez threw three of his trademark jabs, but following the last punch, his arms began to drop. Orlando, taking advantage of this opening, blasted an overhand right to the jaw that snapped Vasquez's head back. Orlando followed with a second blow that sent the champ crashing to the floor.

"This is the first time Antonio Vasquez, the undefeated heavyweight champion of the world, has ever been knocked off his feet," shouted the silver-haired commentator, but his voice could hardly be heard above the tumult of the near-hysterical crowd.

Stunned and humiliated, Vasquez rose slowly but determinedly by the count of seven and was startled to see Orlando jumping back into the fray like an enraged mountain lion pursuing a rabbit. The challenger poured out a withering string of heavy overhead rights until, after three in a row connected, Vasquez dropped to his knees, his neck so weak and rubber-like that he could hardly hold his head in one place.

This time he was barely standing by the count of nine when

Orlando was on top of him again. With eight breathless seconds left in the round, the challenger delivered a blow, and its impact could be felt to the farthest reaches of the arena. The champ reeled backward like a felled tree but, knowing full well that a third knockdown would have ended the fight, somehow managed to remain on his feet by clinging desperately to the ropes. At that moment, seeing his chance, Orlando rushed in to finish the job he had started, but it was too late. The bell rang, and the round was over.

At the halfway point of the match, Orlando was clearly ahead on points. So far he'd won all the rounds 10–9, and he had definitely won the last one with those two knockdowns. But points wouldn't be enough to carry him through the rest of the match, since the younger Vasquez would likely regain his strength. As Orlando returned to his corner, Sugar Ray immediately sensed the desperate situation Orlando was in. That vital sixth-round knockout had evaded him. He was in for the long haul, but the energy he had expended in trying to take the champ out had left him totally drained. Orlando sat on his stool, worn out, panting heavily, and clearly worried about how he would find the energy and focus to continue. He might have won the first half of the fight decisively, but the match was far from over. It was, Sugar Ray knew as well as everyone else gathered around the fighter's corner, a matter of simple mathematics. Orlando's age had stolen the last ounce of power he needed to take the champ down. The champ's youth had given him the vital extra measure of stamina to endure the beating and return with enough reserves to administer some punishment of his own.

Over the course of Round Seven, Orlando tried desperately to repeat his incredible performance in the sixth. But it was evident that the tide was turning in favor of Vasquez and his hammering assault. Although Orlando had been able to call up enough power for one more all-out assault, even knocking the champ to one knee with a flash overhand right, by the end of Round Seven there was a clear shift in the momentum as the weight and youth of Vasquez began to make the difference. Still, with the knockdown Orlando walked away with a 10–8 round.

What followed was painful and excruciating to see. As a horrified Alicia watched and a terrified Darla hid her eyes, Orlando absorbed a savage beating over three brutal rounds from the champ's ruthless and methodical fists. Vasquez concentrated now on an expert sequence of body punches, and a blinding sequence of hard and quick blows raised ugly red welts along the lines of Orlando's abdomen and ribs. Vicious punches to the head opened up cuts along his lips and brows. His eyes began to swell, and the longer the beatings lasted, the slower his response time became until, by the end of the tenth round, he had become little more than Vasquez's punching bag, a helpless victim left to the merciless attack of the heavyweight.

Realizing that his opponent had nothing left to threaten him with, Vasquez worked overtime to take him out for good. Every punch that Vasquez threw was delivered with bad intentions and had knockout written all over it. Only Orlando's long training in the ring and his innate ability to slip in punches like nobody else could kept him from absorbing the most deadly of the champ's well-aimed blows.

At the end of the tenth round, Orlando staggered to his corner and collapsed onto his stool as the trainers did their best to stanch the bleeding from his face and dress the wounds of his body.

"You've taken enough," shouted Sugar Ray above the roaring crowd. "Let's call this thing and go home, Orlando!"

"No," replied Orlando between swollen lips. "Whatever

happens, Ray, don't call it." He looked up at his friend through bloodshot eyes. "Promise me."

"But, Orlando," protested Simon as he rubbed the fighter's shoulders, "you've outlasted every fighter that Vasquez has ever unloaded on. You can't take it anymore. Even George Foreman couldn't absorb this kind of punishment. You've made your point!"

"No!" shouted Orlando, wincing at the pain that even speaking caused him. "You don't get it. I'm not here to make a point. I can't lose now. I've come too far!"

The bell announcing the beginning of Round Eleven sounded to Orlando's ears like the grim tolling of a funeral bell as he staggered to his feet and moved out slowly and painfully to confront more punishment. Vasquez, by contrast, looked as if he had suddenly caught his second wind. He appeared fresh and eager as he danced and wove around the exhausted challenger, taunting and teasing him with feints and exploratory jabs.

Orlando blocked a sudden powerful right in the nick of time, and once again the two fighters grabbed each other in a lockup. The referee moved in to break it up, but Orlando appeared to be using Vasquez's solid bulk just to hold himself up. Finally able to pry them apart, the referee separated them at arm's length and then stepped back, letting the fight continue.

At ringside Alicia seemed to be feeling every blow that landed on her husband's bruised and battered body. "No!" she shouted loudly. "Please! Stop!" Darla, meanwhile, had uncovered her eyes and was watching the bloody spectacle with rapt attention. The child's eyes were wide, but her face was calm, as if she were listening to a calming voice inside her head.

Taking his time, measuring the distance, Vasquez delivered a fully extended overhand right, the precise punch that Sugar Ray had warned Orlando about. This time there was no question of withstanding the stunning blow. Orlando's head snapped back, his neck muscles giving out, and he pitched forward, landing face first on the canvas.

"Orlando!" shouted Alicia as the referee began the count and Orlando tried to rise, but he could get only as far as his hands and knees, crawling around the canvas in a daze.

"One. Two." Each count was marked by a swing of the referee's arm. "Three. Four."

From the champ's corner, Freddie was suddenly on his feet, shouting for his brother to get up, even as Sam Freeman fixed him with a shocked and angry look.

Surrounded by the horrified faces of the kids from the youth center, Geneva was on her feet, shouting and weeping. "Stay down, son!" she begged. "Stay down and let it end!"

"Five. Six. Seven." The count continued as the champ held up his arms in anticipation of victory. "Eight. Nine."

At that moment a strange power surged through Orlando's body, straightening his spine and giving strength to his buckling knees. As if an invisible power had reached under his arms to lift him upright, he used the ropes to pull himself off of the mat and stood, bloody but unbowed, before the amazed Vasquez. The roar of the crowd redoubled as even those who had come to cheer on the champ saw in Orlando a different kind of hero, a man who would not give up.

"This is incredible," the older reporter was screaming into the microphone. "The crowd is going absolutely berserk!"

"If I had to make a prediction right now," said his partner, "I'd have to say that on points, if Orlando can miraculously finish this fight—and I do mean if—it could be a close one on the scorecards, given Orlando's early lead. The champ has obviously had the advantage over these past six rounds. I'm sure he wanted to score a clean knockout to ensure victory. But Leone is hanging on by sheer willpower! This man is showing superhuman endurance!"

At last the bell closing the eleventh round sounded, and Orlando returned to his corner, for all intents and purposes a completely defeated fighter. His eyes were swollen almost entirely shut, and the bruises on his upper body were so numerous his torso looked as if a truck had run over it. Far from looking forty, he seemed to have aged twenty years in the past hour, and there was no question among those gathered in his corner that stopping the fight was the only logical alternative to this virtual human sacrifice.

"No way," Orlando croaked when Simon put the question to him again. "Not now. Not until it's finished."

With a helpless look to Sugar Ray, the pastor signaled the officials that the fighter wanted to continue.

For Orlando, the arena and everyone in it had faded into a red blur. He knew where he was and he knew his purpose in being there, but beyond that, all that existed was the world of pain that seemed to have been his habitation for as long as he could remember. A voice in his brain told him that in a few more minutes it would all be over, but it might as well have been telling him that the agony he was enduring would last forever. Time had stopped. There was no end to the violence being inflicted on him. His only choice was to take his chances and try to endure to the end.

As the roar of the crowd seemed to fade in his ears, the sweetest, purest sound that he had ever heard reached him as if on a gently wafting breeze. He turned his head, feeling every strained muscle in his neck, and saw, there below him at ringside, Darla standing on her chair and lifting her small voice against the surging tide of humanity around her. The song was "Amen," and it brought with it a blessing to Orlando like a deep, soothing balm to his tattered flesh.

Slowly, one by one, the members of the youth center choir joined in the melody, and within moments their glorious harmonies were reaching up to heaven. But the miracle didn't stop there. As the people quieted, curiously at first to hear such a sound in such a place, they began to join in until the arena resounded with thousands of voices. What had been a carnival of violence and brutality was transformed into a holy war, with nearly ten thousand people singing the old Negro spiritual over and over. Orlando, at the head of the heavenly host, was leading them on to victory.

Suddenly rising to his feet, Orlando felt a piercing light of God's presence touch his spirit. A fresh determination flooded him, and his body at that moment seemed to belong to someone else. For a moment he became the greatest fighter in the world, a champion who had never been defeated and never would be, whether in or out of the ring. As the bell rang, announcing the twelfth and final round, Orlando felt himself move back into the ring, alive with the certain knowledge that, no matter what happened now, he was in the exact center of God's will.

While the crowd continued singing, Orlando easily dodged every shot the champ sent his way, answering each one with an accurate and well-placed jab of his own. More than having a second wind, Orlando seemed to be borne up by a hurricane-strength gust of pure power and brilliant fighting technique.

"I've never seen anything like this before," remarked the stunned older sportscaster. "The entire arena seems to have broken into song, no doubt being spurred on by the members of Leone's youth center who are gathered here tonight."

"Whatever and whoever it is," marveled his partner, "it's given the challenger a powerful new incentive to finish this fight. This last-round comeback is one for the record books!"

Freddie stared at the heroic figure of his brother in the ring. Tears filled his eyes, and for the first time in his life, he spoke out a prayer. "Please, God," he begged, "protect him up there."

"What did you say?" demanded an enraged Freeman, who had jumped up next to him.

"I asked God to save my brother's life!" Freddie shouted defiantly.

In the ring, Orlando delivered a series of devastating blows to the champ. Vasquez reeled back into the ropes and, for a moment, seemed as if he were about to fall. But instead, with a bellow like a gored bull, he rushed back at his opponent. Like a demonic machine, he blasted away with his iron fists to the body until Orlando, dazed and winded, dropped to his knees.

"One. Two," the referee began again, his count drowned by the singing that reverberated off the walls. Orlando rose to his feet, blood streaming down his face from a new cut above his eye. Somehow, with an effort that seemed to well up from someplace deep inside his heart, Orlando raised his fists to face his foe. Once again the champ gave him his best shot, a devastating blow to the jaw that seemed to echo through the arena, and once again Orlando went down. "One. Two," the count started again, and for those high in the cheap seats of the arena, it seemed as if the very roof of the building was in danger of lifting off and being blown away by the sheer volume of human voices.

With a groan that seemed to signal his last ounce of strength being tapped, Orlando rose to his feet as the song reached a deafening crescendo, and the champ pulled back his arm for the hardest, most direct and unmerciful blow of the entire fight. As he threw it, Orlando ducked under it and responded with an uppercut that came from somewhere near his knees and exploded under

Vasquez's chin, literally lifting him off the canvas. As he came back down, he fell against the top half of the ropes, which—like a sling shot—catapulted him toward the center of the ring, where he landed hard on his face and chest.

"Orlando! Orlando! Orlando!" chanted the crowd in unison. Orlando smiled to himself. Vasquez was humiliated in this obvious moment of glory for the challenger. Surprising to everyone, though, Vasquez got up quickly and, spinning around, took the mandatory eight-count. He charged at Orlando, only to find that Leone still had fifteen seconds of glory left.

Orlando threw three jabs, which landed flush on Vasquez's face, followed by two right-left-right-left combinations that also landed squarely and snapped the champ's head back. Then, to the surprise and enjoyment of the crowd, Orlando somehow found in his forty-year-old legs one last "Ali Shuffle," followed by a hard overhand right that dropped Vasquez on the seat of his pants. The whole arena laughed and cheered as he got to his feet by the count of three. Fortunately for him, the bell rang and his nightmare was over.

The bell rang. The fight was over. Orlando was still standing, even as a team of first aid medics rushed to him and began dressing his wounds. An eerie silence descended on the arena as the crowd waited for the judges' decision. Even the sportscasters could find no words to describe the electric tension that hung in the air.

At last the announcer, dressed in a white shirt and black bow tie, climbed into the ring, carrying a piece of paper. The microphone was lowered, and the absolute silence continued as he read the results.

"Ladies and gentlemen," he said, his voice booming, "we have a split decision. Judge Alby Shirley scores the bout 113 to 112 in favor of Vasquez. Judge John Warren scores the bout 113 to 110, Leone." He paused, and across the arena, the audience held its collective breath. "Judge Al Ledderman scores the bout 113 to 112, to the winner by split decision, the new heavyweight champion of the world, Orlando Leone Jr.!"

Whatever ear-splitting noise the crowd had been able to generate up to that point was doubled in response to the announcement, drowning out Orlando's name as soon as the word *new* rang through the air. At ringside, Alicia collapsed into her chair, weeping openly as her daughter hugged her tightly. On the other side of the mat, Freddie leaped up and down in ecstasy as a furious Freeman tore up his program and hurled the pieces at the floor. The air was thick with paper and debris as spectators began to flood the ring, and in the aisles, the youth center teens began executing an intricately choreographed victory dance.

In the ring, the dazed Orlando, battered and bloody, suddenly found himself back in his body, partaking fully of the pain and agony that it had been subjected to. When the beaming announcer handed him the heavyweight championship belt, it felt like an unbearable load of lead in his exhausted arms, but with his last ounce of strength he lifted it high over his head.

Then Orlando felt himself being lifted by the jubilant crowd as they carried him out of the ring and up the aisle toward the back of the arena. Although he couldn't be exactly sure, he could have sworn in that moment he saw his father, Papa Leone, smiling proudly at him from a ringside seat. As the crowd set him down, Simon and Sugar Ray were next to him, holding him up on each side and half dragging him toward the locker room door. It was then that he saw his brother, Freddie, clearing a path through the crowd for him to walk and turning back to nod approvingly at his kid brother.

On the other side of the arena, Vasquez was surrounded by reporters, all clamoring for a comment on his devastating loss. A new light of respect had dawned in the former champion's eyes, and as he gestured for silence, he felt a lump in his throat. "Orlando Leone is a man of great strength and great faith," he said, choking back his emotions. "It was an honor to be in the ring with him. I've never had a more worthy opponent in my career, and I want to be the first to congratulate him on a hard-fought victory."

"Thank you, gentlemen," said his trainer as he stepped between the boxer and the press. "That'll be all."

A similar scene was being enacted outside the door of Orlando's locker room, but with an even larger assembly of reporters, all shouting questions at the same time to the dazed and bloodied champ.

When he began to speak, it was in a voice so low that the crowd immediately quieted in order to hear his words. "It's over," he said in a hoarse whisper. "I never wanted to fight in the first place, but since I had to, I want to thank my Lord and Savior, Jesus Christ, for giving me the strength to run this race."

"What about a rematch?" several reporters shouted at once.

Orlando shook his head weakly. "No rematch, guys," he said with a slight smile. "I've finished my course."

The crush of reporters, cameras, and microphones threatened to pin Orlando, Simon, and Sugar Ray to the wall, but Freddie pushed them back. Only when he turned around to face his brother again did he realize that Orlando had lost consciousness, his head resting on his shoulder and his eyes closed.

CHAPTER TWENTY

TWO BURLY SECURITY GUARDS ESCORTED ALICIA AND DARLA down the long corridor that led to Orlando's locker room. As they approached, the reporters lingering at the door, several of the newshounds who had been on the story from the beginning, jumped up and ran toward them, recognizing the new champ's wife and stepdaughter. But the guards brushed them away and, clearing a path through the thicket of microphones and cameras, made sure they got safely inside.

The scene that awaited them caused Alicia to go pale and Darla to let out a small cry of fear. Orlando was surrounded by medics who were working like a well-integrated team to revive him. As they stood watching in horror, the head emergency medical technician signaled for the others to stand back.

"We've got to get him into intensive care," he said in a somber tone of voice. "Now."

Within seconds two men carrying a stretcher had burst into the room, and with the utmost care, the team transferred Orlando off the massage table.

"Where are you taking him?" Alicia demanded to know, and the head EMT called out the name of a nearby hospital. Grabbing her daughter by the hand, she hurried out, trailing the stretcher bearers down the hall until they emerged into the cool night air of the parking lot.

The large crowd that had gathered at the exit door waiting for a glimpse of the new heavyweight world champion set up a cheer as Orlando was carried into the back of a waiting ambulance. As Alicia and Darla climbed in next to him, a figure emerged from the crowd and pushed his way past the security guards.

"It's okay," shouted Alicia as the guards tried to restrain Freddie. "It's Orlando's brother!" She looked out the back door of the ambulance into the stricken face of her brother-in-law. "Meet us at the hospital," she told him. "And bring the others with you." Freddie nodded, wide-eyed, as the door was shut and the ambulance took off, its siren wailing and the red light on its roof casting a garish glow over the crowd.

Twenty minutes later, Freddie pushed through the double doors of the hospital's main entrance followed closely by Pete, Sugar Ray, and Geneva. Sprinting to the front desk, he identified himself and got his brother's room number. Rushing to the elevator, the four were grimly silent as they rode to the intensive care floor, each lost in silent thoughts and fervent prayers.

Alicia and Darla were sitting at Orlando's bedside when the rest of his family and friends arrived. His wife was holding his hand tightly, peering anxiously into his face, barely visible through its wrapping of bandages. Machines monitoring his vital signs clicked and beeped softly, but the atmosphere in the room seemed strangely peaceful. As the others crowded around the bedside, Orlando's eyes opened. The first person he saw was his brother.

"Hey, Freddie," he said, his voice barely audible. "Sorry I smacked you in the head the other day." He laughed weakly, then winced with pain.

Freddie took a step closer. "Don't worry about it, kid," he replied. "I had it coming." He leaned in close. "I'm just glad you had something left over for Vasquez."

"You sure did," agreed Sugar Ray, stepping into Orlando's field of vision. "That was the most incredible fight I've ever seen, buddy." He smiled. "I'm just glad it wasn't me you were going up against."

"I could have used your legs out there tonight," Orlando told him in a whisper. "Especially after that seventh round. It was like I had Hagler, Hearns, and Duran all chasing me around at the same time."

"And believe me," replied Sugar Ray, "I know what that's like."

Orlando turned his head slowly, meeting the gaze of each and every person in the room, stopping finally with his mother. "Mom," he told Geneva, "I need to have a little time alone with my family."

"Of course you do, son," she said, fighting back tears, then clapped her hands briskly. "You heard the man," she said to the others. "He needs his time." She turned back to him. "We'll just be outside if you need anything," she managed to get out before turning to hide her tears.

In the hallway outside the door, Sugar Ray stopped a passing doctor and asked for an update on Orlando's condition. "How bad is it, Doc?" he asked confidentially, trying to shield the rest from the bad news he feared might be coming.

The doctor shook his head. "It's not good," he said in the straightforward manner that comes from dealing with life-and-death issues on a daily basis. "He has six broken ribs, most of which have punctured vital organs. We've tried everything we can, but there's no way to stop the internal hemorrhaging." He leaned in closer. "I think you had better prepare for the worst. It could be tonight. Tomorrow morning at the latest." Sugar Ray turned, only to find the others gathered close, their faces collapsing into grief at the doctor's words.

"It's time to start praying," Geneva said.

On the other side of the door, Alicia and Darla remained at their bedside vigil. "Mommy," Darla asked in a low whisper, "is Daddy going to be all right?"

"We need to pray, Darla," Alicia told her daughter. "We need to pray very hard."

Regaining consciousness, Orlando smiled at the little girl. "Come up here, sweetheart," he told her, and Darla climbed onto the bed and wrapped her arms around him.

"I want you to listen very closely, Darla," he told her in a pained and hoarse whisper. "I want you to know that the only reason I was able to win that fight was because you were there by my side. You gave me the strength to go on, sweetheart, and now I want you to be able to give that same strength to your mom. She needs someone to take care of her. Someone to love her as much as I do."

Darla began to cry, holding on even tighter around Orlando's neck.

"Honey," Alicia said, "you're hurting him."

"No," Orlando replied. "It's okay." He stroked Darla's head and said softly to her, "Honey? I want you to go out into the hallway and get Uncle Freddie for me. Can you do that for Daddy?"

Darla nodded and, hopping off the bed, ran out the door. A moment later she was back, holding Freddie by the hand.

"You got it?" he asked his brother, and Freddie slipped an envelope into his trembling hands. The two embraced. "Thanks," Orlando said at last. "Thanks for everything."

"No, kid," replied Freddie through tears, "thank you. You've taught me so much. And given me a way back into the family. There's no way I can repay you for that."

Orlando nodded and drew his brother close. "I'll tell Dad you said hello when I see him," he said.

Unable to endure the sorrow for a moment longer, Freddie took Darla by the hand and returned to the hallway to wait for the inevitable with the others.

For a long moment the silence between Alicia and Orlando remained unbroken. "Just you and me, babe," Orlando said at last.

"I'll be right here," Alicia promised. "And when you get out, you're going to have the two best nurses in the world. Darla and I will—"

Orlando reached up and put a finger over her lips. "Shhhh," he said, quieting her. "I want you to know something," he said, his voice dropping very low. "I'll always love you, Alicia. Nothing can ever change that. That's something I want you to remember, always."

"Don't talk like that, Orlando," she pleaded. "You're going to be just fine."

He shook his head, his eyes bright and a joyful smile on his face. "No," he said, "I'm going home. It's my time."

"I won't let you," she sobbed, holding on to him tightly and wetting his face with her tears.

"Alicia," he said softly, stroking her hair, "my spirit is ready. The Lord is calling me. My dad's there, waiting for me."

"But that's not faith," she replied in anguish. "You've got to believe that you'll get better, Orlando. There's so much left for you to do. The youth center needs you. I need you. Who's going to turn that hospital into what you dreamed it would become? Who'll raise the money? It'll take years to get the millions we need. You can't talk like this—only you can accomplish this. You said that God promised you it would come to pass. You said building this center was your purpose in life." The tears glistened on her cheeks now as she clutched his hand and brought it to her lips, kissing it over and over. "You can't leave us! We need you here."

Orlando soothed her, speaking softly into her ear and touching her cheek with a gentle brush of his fingers. "Some things are out of our hands, sweetheart," he said, even now feeling his life energies beginning to fade. "But everything's going to be fine. I took care of it."

"What do you mean?" asked Alicia, her head resting on his shoulder.

"Remember when I said I had a couple of favors to ask?" he continued. She nodded. "Well, one of those favors is in that envelope. You see, I couldn't understand why God was putting me through this ordeal until Darla said God was with me, the devil against me, and my vote decided the election . . . Well . . . that's when it clicked. You see, if God was on my side, that meant it was a sure thing. If He believed in me, that meant I could believe in myself. So I told Freddie to do me a favor. I asked him to bet my purse on me to win the fight. I was going to take home a million dollars, win or lose. The odds against me were twenty to one. So, if I won the fight—even on points—I could turn the million into twenty million. Which is exactly enough to complete the renovation on the hospital." He gently turned her face to him. "I'm moving on," he said, looking deep into her eyes. "This is your job now. Like my dad passed it on to me, I'm passing it on to you. I know you can do it."

He coughed and closed his eyes. Without words, without any

sign passing between them, the husband and the wife knew the time of their parting was near.

"Orlando," Alicia sobbed, "I love you so much."

With the last of his ebbing strength, Orlando smiled up at her. "Remember the song?" he said in a barely audible voice. "The one I wrote for Darla? Well, now it's for you too." With scarcely enough life left to draw breath, Orlando began to sing in her ear softly, with a weakened voice.

I'll always love you.
I'll always care.
You are the one love to whom none compare.
When skies are gray and friends are untrue,
I'll be that someone who'll watch over you.
When life is over,
When all's said and done,
You will have always been my number one—

Suddenly Orlando stopped and told Alicia, "Hold me."

She reached through the tubes and heart monitor wires and hugged him warmly, yet firmly. "What is it, Orlando?"

He gently said, "I want to hold the one I love the most as I leave." Then he closed his eyes. His thick, bruised arms went limp, and Orlando slipped from one dimension into the next. Alicia held him with her face buried in his chest and cried.

EPILOGUE

A REFRESHING SPRING RAIN FELL GENTLY ON THE CROWD
that had gathered outside the building for the dedication. Crowded
into the parking lot, the entire neighborhood seemed to have
turned out as well as a huge press corps and several of city hall's
most important dignitaries. Behind them rose the gleaming, state-
of-the-art edifice of the former hospital, transformed now into a
beautiful and immaculate new youth center.

Under a wide umbrella, Sugar Ray, Geneva, and Pete greeted
the distinguished guests and the members of the community who
had gathered for the event. Standing on a podium under the
awning of the youth center's side entry, Alicia was dressed ele-
gantly for the occasion. Darla was at her side. After the band
behind her completed a rendition of "'Tis So Sweet to Trust in
Jesus," Alicia stepped up to the microphone and cleared her throat.

"Ladies and gentlemen," she announced, "may I have your
attention, please?" The crowd quieted as all eyes turned to the
widow of the late heavyweight champion of the world. "In such
moments," she began, speaking from the heart without notes,
"moments that define the life of a community, we must pause to
give thought to those whose sacrifices made such accomplish-
ments as this great building possible." She gestured behind her as

the crowd applauded. Holding up her hands for silence, she continued, "It was over thirty years ago that such a man, Orlando Leone Sr., walked these very streets, spreading the good news of Jesus Christ through his music, his words, and the example of his life."

Alicia turned to smile at her daughter, who was watching her mother proudly. "It was two years ago that I myself heard that good news and met my Savior face-to-face through the words and the example of another unsung hero of this neighborhood, Orlando Leone Jr. Orlando demonstrated many of the same traits as his namesake, and I'm sure most of you will remember him as a leader, as a friend, or maybe you just knew him as the champ. But however we best knew him, God knew my husband as a dedicated servant, willing to give all to fulfill the purpose he had been given in life."

She turned around and looked up at the towering edifice of the building. "This beautiful new center is the fulfillment of that purpose," she continued. "This is your center, a gift from Orlando Leone, a place of recreation, a sanctuary for unwed mothers, a home for the homeless, a school to teach our children the Word of God, a haven for saints, and a house of forgiveness for sinners. Ladies and gentlemen, I now present to you the Orlando Leone Jr. Youth Center!"

Wave after wave of cheers and applause followed her words, and several long minutes passed before Alicia could once again hold the audience's attention. "Before we open the doors and invite you in for a visit to this wonderful new facility," she said, "I would like to tell you something that I think Orlando himself might have said if he could have been here with us today." She stopped, waiting for the welling tears in her eyes to subside. "He would want you all to know that if today you want to make your life right before God, if you want to ask the Lord to forgive your past life and give you a brand-new future, then there is an altar inside that will be open for the first time for you to make that commitment. This is your day. A day of new beginnings. A day of new birth." She bowed her head. "I think Orlando would have wanted us to sing a song of praise to our God and pray for this place and the people who will come through its doors by the thousands in all the years to come."

Behind her, the choir began the gentle, soaring harmonies of "'Tis So Sweet to Trust in Jesus." The doors of the center were flung open, and people from every walk of life and all conditions of sin and salvation made their way inside. Street people, gang members, and prostitutes mingled with businessmen, homemakers, and shopkeepers. Even many of the reporters and cameramen join the impromptu procession.

As Alicia watched the multitudes file slowly in, the clouds parted and rays of bright sunlight bathed the building. From the rear of the crowd she recognized a familiar figure. As Freddie smoked a cigarette, his expensive suit and Italian shoes soaked with rain, he walked slowly but with determination toward the open doors. From where she stood it was hard for Alicia to tell whether it was raindrops or tears that wet her brother-in-law's face.

When Freddie entered the center, his eyes fell on a bust that stood outside the front door of the building. It was of a man who looked a lot like his father, but without the mustache and glasses, even more like his brother. As a matter of fact, it was his brother. Alicia had changed the name and the likeness to that of Orlando's. Beneath the lifelike sculpture was a simple inscription. Wiping the tears from his eyes, he stopped to read its words:

Greater love hath no man than this,
that a man lay down his life for his friends.
                                        —John 15:13

He looked up at the face and softly slapped the cheek the way he used to when he and Orlando were kids. "Well, little brother," he said, "You finally got to me. Tell Pop not to worry about Freddie . . . I'm in." He threw his cigarette on the ground, stomping it out, and walked up to where Alicia was. He hugged her and said, "I'll take care of things . . . I'm home now."

CONTACT INFORMATION

• • •

Carman Ministries
P.O. Box 5093
Brentwood, TN 37024
Phone: (615) 771-2711
Fax: (615) 771-2722
www.carman.org

Management:
Rendy Lovelady Management
1102 17th Avenue South
Suite 402
Nashville, TN 37211
Phone: (615) 340-9500
Fax: (615) 340-9505

Booking:
Creative Artist Agency
3310 West End Avenue
5th Floor
Nashville, TN 37203
Phone: (615) 383-8787
Fax: (615) 383-4937

Personal Appearance/TV:
Creative Artist Agency
9830 Wilshire Blvd.
Beverly Hills, CA 90212
Phone: (310) 288-4545
Fax: (310) 288-4800